Cathy couldn't believe what was happening!

Scanning Cathy's stunned face with bitter pleasure, Jake's sister laughed. "You've lost, Cathy. Both of them. Jake as well as my husband. Only you never really had Jake—"

"That's enough!" Jake told his sister coldly.

His voice cut off the poisonous diatribe. The woman hesitated. "Jake?" she said uncertainly. Her eyes searched his impassive face, half ashamed, half pleading.

Then she turned toward Cathy.

"You see, Cathy," she continued acidly. "My husband has always thought that deep down you were in love with him. I had to let him discover you in bed with someone else. Fortunately, Jake was available."

Cathy willed herself to conceal the slashing torment she suddenly felt at the news of Jake's betrayal....

ROBYN DONALD lives in northern New Zealand with her husband and children. They love the outdoors and particularly enjoy sailing and stargazing on warm nights. Robyn doesn't remember being taught to read, but rates reading as one of her greatest pleasures, if not a vice. She finds writing intensely rewarding and is continually surprised by the way her characters develop independent lives of their own.

Books by Robyn Donald

Don't miss any of our special offers. Write to us at the following address for information on our newest releases.

Harlequin Reader Service
901 Fuhrmann Blvd., P.O. Box 1397, Buffalo, NY 14240
Canadian address: P.O. Box 603,
Fort Erie, Ont. L2A 5X3

ROBYN DONALD

love's reward

Harlequin Books

TORONTO • NEW YORK • LONDON
AMSTERDAM • PARIS • SYDNEY • HAMBURG
STOCKHOLM • ATHENS • TOKYO • MILAN

Harlequin Presents first edition January 1990
ISBN 0-373-11233-5

Original hardcover edition published in 1989
by Mills & Boon Limited

CHAPTER ONE

THE persistent ring of the security bell finally penetrated far enough through Cathy Durrant's dreams to wake her. Yawning, she pushed a mass of tumbled red hair back from her small face to peer with outraged eyes at the clock on her bedside table. One-thirty! Who on earth could be wanting her at this hour of the morning, for heaven's sake!

But two years spent working in an orphanage had inured her to waking up at ungodly hours. Muttering grumpily, she climbed out of bed and pulled a robe around her slender body, her fingers clutching the cream satin in an apprehension she would not express.

'Yes?' she said starkly into the communications system.

'For God's sake, Cathy, let me in. It's bloody cold out here.'

'Peter! What——? Oh, all right, all right . . .' She pressed the button which released the street door and waited for his peremptory knock, hiding another yawn with her hand.

Peter Theobald was her very oldest friend, the boy next door who had been kind to his adoring little neighbour even when she grew up to be a spoilt brat; they knew each other better than most brothers and sisters. So when he slammed in through the door she eyed him with less apprehension than resignation, sighing silently as she realised he had been drinking.

'I'll make some coffee,' she said, turning towards the kitchen.

He grabbed her arm, his fingers biting into the soft flesh. 'I'm not drunk.'

'I know, but if you'll excuse me for saying it, I'm going to need something to keep me awake. I presume you came here for a reason.'

Shamefaced, he released her, his outrageously handsome face contorting into an expression of self-disgust. 'I'm sorry, Cathy, it's just that there's no one else.'

It was the one explanation which made an instant impact. With a wry, commiserating smile, she said, 'Yes, I know. Come and tell me about it while I make the coffee.'

But once in the smart grey and white kitchen he seemed unable to begin. As her hands deftly measured coffee grounds into the pot Cathy watched him from beneath her lashes. He prowled back and forth, his face twisting and his movements jerky and uncoordinated, until she put the coffee on a tray and led the way into the sitting-room. Then he collapsed into an armchair and said defeatedly, 'It's Emma.'

Biting back the impulse to observe acidly that it was always Emma, Cathy put two lumps of sugar into his cup and stirred it before handing it over.

'Thank you,' he said absently. He stared down into it for a moment before blurting out, 'At least, it's that bloody brother of hers. The great Jake Ferrers, playwright and novelist *extraordinaire*, darling of the literati, golden boy of the masses, sophisticated man of the world, devil with the ladies, the twentieth century's answer to Shakespeare! It's not as though I didn't tell her! She knew that life in New Zealand with a struggling lawyer wasn't going to be as glamorous as living with a man so famous, but she said she was tired of the shallowness of it all. And all she's done since we got married is compare me to him.'

His mouth twisted. For a moment he looked like the small boy of the photographs in Cathy's album, terrifyingly vulnerable. A wrench of pain squeezed her heart, but she knew better than to offer overt sympathy. This was the second time he had turned up late at night since she arrived home after two years spent overseas and she knew that it was only when things became unbearable that he sought refuge. Like all children of possessive parents, like Cathy herself, he had learned to hide his emotions in case they were exploited.

Now he looked up at her, the pain in his eyes stark and open. 'I'm not like him. I'm never going to be like him,' he said in a slurred, hopeless voice. 'You haven't met him, have you? You were still looking after kids in that jungle when we got married. He's—well, he's like some bloody paragon, tall and good-looking and confident, and you only have to look at him to know he's the sort of man you never forget. He's a natural leader. Men respect him and women swoon over him. He's arrogant and he can be bloody nasty but he's fair. I like him. And I am sick to death of having him cast in my teeth every time I don't catch a waiter's eye or I have to tell my wife we can't afford a dress that's just come in from Paris. She wanted to fly over to Sydney to buy clothes and have dinner with old friends!'

Cathy, who could fly anywhere she wanted to in the world without worrying about the cost, said quietly, 'She sounds unhappy, Pete.'

'She probably is.' He sneered the words, as though he hated the woman he had married a year ago. 'Unhappy because she can't waste money, because I can't give her the sort of social life she's used to. Auckland doesn't compare with London or New York or Rio. But she knew, Cathy, she knew that! I told her, spelled it out, and she accepted it! She said it didn't matter, that she loved me . . .'

He bit his lip and took a deep breath. In an unsteady raw voice he finished, 'But she doesn't. She wanted someone who'll measure up to her brother so she can preen and gloat because she's snaffled a great prize from under the noses of all the other women who want him. That's what she wants, and I'll never get there. Jake's one on his own. It's as simple as that.'

Cathy felt totally inadequate. In spite of a short-lived marriage five years ago when she was an extraordinarily naïve eighteen, she had little experience on which to base any attempt at consolation. Her father had been killed when she was barely old enough to remember him and her grandparents' marriage had been the traditional sort where her grandfather was very definitely in charge. Her own marriage had been quite literally a non-event.

Cautiously she suggested, 'Are you sure, Peter? Surely she must have known——'

'She was infatuated.' He suddenly drank down the coffee and set the cup and saucer on to the table with a small crash. 'Sex,' he said in a blurred voice. 'That's all it was. It's still great——'

'You shouldn't be telling me this.' The interruption was sharp and decided.

He stared owlishly at her then gave a lopsided smile. 'Funny little Cath,' he said affectionately. 'So prim and proper. Your grandmother did a job on you, didn't she. You know, I've often wondered just what happened in that marriage of yours. You came out of it just the same as you went in, still repressed, as though ol' Trent never touched you.'

Cathy bit back a swift, heartfelt comment. Fond though she was of Peter, she had no intention of discussing her marriage with anyone, not even him. She said tartly. 'You'd better go home. Emma will be worried stiff. You aren't driving, are you?'

'Nope,' he said cheerfully, closing his eyes and sinking back into the chair. 'You know, if you hadn't tol' me with your own mouth that you blackmailed Trent Addison into marrying you, I'd never have believed you. Not 'cause you wouldn't have done it. You were game enough to take anyone on. Used to envy you, you know. No nerves, no fear . . .'

'I was a spoiled little beast!' Desperate to get him off the subject of the most humiliating experience of her life, one she still couldn't recall without deep shame, she hurried on, 'I'll call a taxi to take you home.'

But he refused to be diverted. He said earnestly, 'No, not surprised you and that pirate of a grandfather forced him to marry you. Clever scheme, arranging for old Sir Peter to find you *in flagrante delicto*, so to speak. And just like the old devil to put pressure on Addison, force him to make an honest woman of you or lose control of his own firm.' He chuckled, opening his eyes to look at her with a bleary amusement. 'But you know, the thing that s'prises me is that Addison didn't make your life hell. Seems to have behaved like a perfect gentleman! Not his reputation, y'know. Just as much a buccaneer as your grandfather. I'd have thought he'd have made you so bloody sorry you trapped him that you never wanted to see him again. But he doesn't seem to bear you any grudges. 'N fact we're all having dinner there tomorrow, so Emma says. She doesn't want to go.' He scowled, momentarily diverted, then said with all the tenacity of the drunk, 'I don't think he ever touched you, did he? You wouldn't be so prissy if he had.'

Cathy said shortly, 'That's none of your business.'

'It's not as if you're not pretty,' he mused, ignoring her. 'And in spite of what Emma thinks, I never had any feelings for you like that, well, stands to reason, doesn't it, we were practically brought up together like brother and sister, but even I can see you're something extra. Lovely,' he finished vaguely. A frown drew his brows together. 'Emma's jealous of you. Says you look obvious. Why won't you let me tell anyone you spent last couple of years working in some jungle in Asia looking after a pack of orphans?'

She could have heaved a sigh of relief. At last he was off the subject of her marriage! 'Because it's no one's business but mine. Anyway, no one would believe you. They're all convinced I've spent my time swanning around the world spending Sir Peter's money and living it up.'

How could she tell anyone that the time spent in the orphanage was some kind of expiation?

'Yes, well, you don't try to change their minds,' he said obstinately. 'Bloody arrogant. You always have been . . .'

Not any more, she thought drily. No, not since Trent Addison had, just by being his chivalrous self, shown her how little she had to be arrogant about. Of course he had never touched her! He had been in love with his Melissa, and when the divorce had come through they had married. But he had never been anything but unfailingly kind to the girl who had blackmailed him into marrying her. Kind, and aloof, freezing her so deeply she sometimes wondered if she was ever going to thaw out.

A snore from the sofa interrupted her unhappy thoughts. Frowning, she ruthlessly shook Peter's shoulder, saying in the hard voice she used to hide emotion, 'Wake up, Pete, you can't go to sleep here! Emma will be worried sick. I'll call you a taxi.'

He opened his eyes at that, announced belligerently, 'I'm not going home any more,' and went back to sleep.

Cathy hesitated, unsure of the best way to handle the situation. He was, she thought sadly, so extraordinarily handsome, even with the contours of his face relaxed and his mouth slightly open! It was no wonder Emma, only twenty, had lost her head over him.

At last, after some thought, she shook him awake enough to get him on to the bed in the second bedroom, removed his shoes and covered him with a blanket, before heading briskly across to the telephone.

The receiver at the other end was lifted immediately and Emma's voice, half fearful, half truculent, answered.

'It's Cathy Durrant here,' Cathy said without preamble. 'Peter will be staying the rest of the night with me. He——'

Emma's voice froze. 'Gloating, are you? Well, you can have him!' and the receiver was crashed down.

Cathy sighed then shrugged her slender shoulders. If Peter was right about his wife's attitude, perhaps a little jealousy might help the situation, but she suspected not. Lifting the receiver she dialled the number again. The ring was abruptly cut off as someone took the handset up but a vicious click in her ear revealed that Emma had severed the connection. Clearly she was not going to answer the telephone any more that night; however, she knew where her husband was and that he was safe.

When Cathy woke the next morning Peter was gone but later that morning as she dressed for her visit to her lawyer a large bouquet of red carnations and white gypsophila was delivered. The card said *Thanks, sweet Kate, Pete.* She stood for a moment looking at the flowers, her expression pensive, then put them in water and left the apartment for her appointment.

An hour later her lawyer, who was also one of the trustees left in charge of the estate willed to her by her grandfather, looked at her with interest nicely mixed with scepticism. 'So you intend to take a degree in business management. What made you decide to do that?'

She smoothed the raw silk of her skirt before shrugging, her brilliant blue eyes very direct although her reply was not. 'My grandmother was very interested in charities for children. The orphanage was very important to her. That's what made me decide to go there to see what was happening. I didn't intend to stay—but they needed help desperately.'

He nodded, shrewd eyes half hidden by his eyelids. He was one of the few people who knew where she had spent all but three months of the last two years.

'Yes,' he murmured, 'Lady Durrant was always most sympathetic towards charities involving children.'

'Possibly because she only had my father and he died so young. While I was working at the orphanage I realised that I was interested in the administrative aspect.' She hesitated, always wary of revealing her emotions, but he nodded and she knew of old that he was totally trustworthy. Encouraged, she went on, choosing her words carefully. 'I loved the children, but I came to see after a while that I could do more for them as an administrator. Besides, I know nothing, nothing about the trust or any of my affairs. My grandfather honestly thought women were unable to understand business——'

She stopped, a faint brush of colour staining her cheeks apricot. A little hastily she finished, 'Not that I don't trust you and Trent, of course, but I don't intend to be a parasite for the rest of my life.'

'I see,' he said softly, and she felt that he did see, perhaps more than she wanted him to. But then he had known her all her life and was privy to all her secrets, except the most shameful. He knew of her possessive mother's attempts to rule her completely, and her final abandonment when she met the steely strength which lay at the core of Cathy's character. She had been sent off to boarding-school; her mother was only interested in people she could dominate.

When a second marriage took Barbara Durrant to America Cathy had been left behind to live with her grandparents. Old Sir Peter had been kind to his granddaughter but he had a chauvinist's attitude towards women, at once contemptuous and paternalistic, and quite deliberately made use of her stupidity to achieve his own ends. Only her gentle grandmother had loved her truly and tried to curb the headstrong wilfulness which, allied to her strong need to be loved, had led to that brief, disastrous marriage to Trent Addison.

She still felt sick when she thought of it. It had taken her years before she could face exactly what she had done to Trent and to the woman he had loved, the woman he was now married to. Trent had never held her headstrong behaviour against her but she knew that Melissa, his wife, was not so forgiving, and she could not blame her for it.

A guilty conscience, Cathy had learned, was a hard taskmaster. Even now she was not looking forward to seeing Melissa Addison again. And somehow it did not make things better to know that when she had realised what she had done Cathy had done her very best to make things right.

She had been so unforgivably immature. These last years had taught her several hard lessons, the most important of which was that it was only when one had a full belly and freedom from bodily pain that one could afford the luxury of emotions beyond the most primitive will to survive.

'So what do you plan to do until the start of the university year?'

She shrugged. 'I want to renew acquaintance with a few people. And then I'm going across to the island for some peace and quiet. The first thing I'm going to do is refurbish the bach.'

They both smiled, because the bach was a far cry from the small seaside house implied by the word. Sir Peter had been in a whimsical mood when he christened the sprawling old farmhouse on its own private beach.

'It probably needs it. No one's stayed there since you left,' the lawyer agreed wryly. 'Who are you going to get in to do it?'

She said coolly, 'I thought I might do it myself. With a little help for the tricky bits.'

'A good idea.' He had the lawyer's trick of speaking in a neutral voice.

Cathy grinned, suddenly mischievous. 'You think I'll make a complete hash of it! Just you wait and see.'

He laughed at that and said, 'My dear, when you look so much like your grandfather I'd be a fool to think anything of the sort. I'm sure you'll be very competent at whatever you do.'

'That's the nicest thing anyone has ever said to me,' she returned in an oddly uneven tone.

She carried the memory of his startled look down to the street with her, smiling like a satisfied child. For once she had surprised him and she was pleased. He knew her well, but he would never understand how important it was to her that she be respected.

Auckland in spring was delightful, with enough warmth in the air to persuade women into the first light clothes of the season. Cathy walked up the street, not hurrying but not strolling either, unaware of the many appreciative glances which slid her way. Pleasure fizzed through her blood, softening the bright blue of her eyes, freeing the sulky curve of her mouth into a half-smile, enigmatic and beckoning. Auckland was her home, and until now she had not realised how much she loved it.

On an impulse she set out for the art gallery and went through the doors into the high modern entrance hall with that same spontaneous anticipatory smile. The main exhibition was a group of statues from the grave mound of the first Chinese Emperor; ever since she had arrived home she had promised herself a viewing, and today seemed the ideal day.

An hour later she was gazing with wondering eyes at the calm, severe face of a life-size statue of a soldier, when from behind her a deep, rather cool voice said, 'Hard to believe that a man who looked like that was a brutal killer, isn't it?'

She was used to men who tried to pick her up, but something in the timbre of the voice interested her and she turned her head. To look up and up and up, into a face slashed with such vibrant implacable masculinity that she almost gasped at the impact of it. And then she was transfixed by eyes of a brilliant blue-green, thoughtful yet speculative as they searched the piquant contours of her face.

It was purely an act of self-defence which twisted her head so that she was free of that unsparing assessment. She felt it still, drawing her, charming her with a forbidden fascination so that she had to clear her throat before she could say in her coolest tone, 'Is that so surprising? I mean—he was a soldier. Even today they're not noted for gentleness.'

'Ah, but he was one of the emperor's crack troops, trained and disciplined with such ferocity that their victories toppled the feudal states of China and placed perhaps the bloodiest autocrat in China's history on the imperial throne. Under the command of an experienced general this man and his fellows were unbeatable. They unified China once and for all, and in the process made themselves and their master so hated that after the fall of his son, a few years after the first emperor's death, a peasant army swarmed through his city destroying everything they could. It's said that the capital burned for three months.'

Her attention caught, she responded, 'I know the first emperor built the great wall and burnt books, but what else did he do that was so terrible?'

He told her, his voice dispassionate as he detailed a history of such cruelty that she was sickened by it and finally broke into the gory recital by asking, 'Are you an expert? You seem to know a lot about him.'

'No, far from an expert. Just interested. You see, he did these things with the very highest of motives. He wanted a strong China, protected from her enemies, with a standard system of weights and measures, coinage, transport, water conservation. The system of government he inaugurated was to serve China well for two thousand years.'

'So you think it was worth it,' she said slowly, thinking that this was a very odd conversation to be having with a total stranger.

He laughed softly. Her eyes were drawn upwards but he was not watching her; there was an ambiguous gleam beneath his heavy lashes as he scrutinised the clay image of the soldier, aloof and serene in the protection of two thousand years. 'In other words, did the end justify the means?' he said, and suddenly, with the impact of a blow, his eyes were back on Cathy's fascinated face, very hard, very aggressive. 'Perhaps. What do you think?'

The thick mass of her hair glowed like swirling fire as she shook her head. She had seen enough of that sort of thinking to last her a lifetime; her grandfather had been an expert at it and following his example had caused her to make the biggest mistake of her life.

'No?' He seemed amused at her decisive answer, and once more those incredible eyes lingered on her face.

Cathy was used to being stared at yet this was something more than the usual sexual appraisal; a finger of ice touched her spine as his gaze slid from her mouth to her suddenly damp temples, and back to her mouth again. For all his blatant appreciation, there was something oblique in that intent survey. Although she felt obscurely threatened, it was impossible to drag her eyes away.

Then his smile widened and she was submerged under a wave of excitement so intense that she took a step backwards without even being aware of it. He chuckled softly and she saw that her instinctive withdrawal had pleased him.

Flattered his ego, she thought waspishly as she allowed her features to set into a cold intimidating mask. She knew what she was feeling; she had been there before. It was this kind of suffocating sexual attraction which had propelled her into her disastrous marriage and she knew, none better, that it was no basis for any kind of relationship except the most superficial.

So in her haughtiest voice she said, 'Thank you for telling me all about the emperor.' And she swung on her heel and walked away, wishing rather fervently that she was tall enough to possess some sort of dignity when she heard his soft, mocking laugher following her.

Back at home she frowned as she caught herself recalling the forceful angularity of his features. Was he handsome? It didn't really matter. He had much more than mere good looks. What made it impossible to banish him from her mind was his blazing vitality and the total self-possession of the man. It made one want to see if there was any way to shatter that armour of confidence.

'Too much,' she said derisively, mocking herself. 'Too much trouble. You've been that way before, Cathy.'

An image of Trent Addison danced beneath her lashes. She had been so sure she loved him that she had blackmailed him into marriage, confident that her love, her desire would be enough. And her youthful arrogance had turned into ashes in her mouth because Trent had proved her wrong.

Her mouth twisted. He could have made her regret her actions with tears and pain, but he had been kind and courteous and pleasant, and implacable. He had never touched her, treating her with a remote courtesy which had first infuriated and then frightened her. For the first time in her life Cathy came up against a man who could not be manipulated.

And slowly she had been forced to realise just how selfish and stupid she had been, how little she had to offer any man in intelligence and character. Pride had stopped her from running to her grandfather, although from somewhere she found the strength to tell him what she had done to Trent. She had been shocked when he'd chuckled and called her a chip off the old block.

Perhaps it was then that she had realised where she was heading. Sir Peter was an old tyrant, more feared and hated than respected. Perhaps only his wife truly loved him. Cathy still didn't know how she felt about him. He had used her, admittedly with her connivance, but nevertheless it hadn't worried him that life in the power of a man who had had to be blackmailed into marrying her had held the seeds of great unhappiness for his only grandchild.

After that Cathy began to ask herself if that was how she wanted to live, continuing to manipulate all who came near her so that she got her own way. Behaving exactly the same way as her mother, she had at last realised.

It was that devastating flash of insight which had set her on a journey lasting two years and which was still far from over.

It had been a long process, this business of learning to understand herself. She smiled a little bitterly, thinking that in many ways life had been simpler when she had arrogantly assumed that just because she wanted something she was entitled to have it.

The gentle purr of the telephone made her start. Frowning, she looked a little vaguely around the expensively furnished room before picking up the receiver.

'Cathy,' a male voice said, and she smiled, her small face irradiated, her voice warming with an intimate, laughing note.

'Trent! How did you know I'd just come in?'

'Intuition,' her ex-husband said cheerfully. 'How are you?'

'I'm very well. How are you? And Melly?'

She could hear the pleasure in his deep voice. 'I am on top of the world, but Melly suffers from morning sickness.'

Just for a moment anguish rippled through her like a lance of fire but she managed to say happily, 'Oh, Trent, how wonderful! Not the morning sickness, it must be hell, but the baby. I don't need to ask how you feel about it, the paternal pride is coming over in waves. Is Melly utterly wretched?'

He laughed. 'For twenty-three hours of the day she's fine. The other hour we don't talk about. She sends her love, by the way.'

Cathy couldn't prevent a grimace from pulling at her mouth. Whatever Melly felt for her, it wasn't love. After all, how could you be fond of the woman who had deprived you of almost three years of happiness? But it was like her to try to make Cathy feel a little less guilty.

Aloud she said, 'Give her my love back and tell her that I think she's so lucky, morning sickness or not. I hope she has a daughter as nice as she is.'

'So,' Trent said gently, 'do I. Now, shall I pick you up tonight? I know you don't like driving at night.'

Carefully refraining from mentioning that she hadn't a car, Cathy returned, 'That was a long time ago! I've grown up now,

Trent, I'm quite capable of driving myself anywhere, at any time.'

She managed to convince him but when she had hung up she stared moodily down at the slender length of her hands on the polished golden wood of the table. The fingernails were short, the natural colour shining healthily through clear varnish. Practical and sensible, where once they had been long, coloured talons. A small sign of the changes the past few years had wrought.

That evening, as she paid the taxi off outside the big house Trent had bought for his wife, she drew a deep shaky breath. It was going to be an ordeal but a necessary one. Only if she came through it successfully would she be really free of the past.

Head held high, she walked up the steps. Trent was there, pirate's face exactly the same, that damned compassion well hidden but ever present. She thought wearily that just once she would like to be accepted by him as a grown woman, and then he smiled and she was able to smile back at him with a sunny radiance which few people had ever seen, her lovely, seductive face fleetingly free from the reserve others mistook for hauteur.

He took her outstretched hand and lifted it to his lips, his shrewd eyes understanding as they held hers.

'All well?'

She nodded and he was satisfied. 'Then come inside and reassure Melly that prospective motherhood hasn't rendered her hideous.'

He was teasing, of course; as always Melly looked stunning, a tall, dark Juno whose lovely smile made every person she met forget immediately that she wasn't conventionally beautiful. Tension darkened Cathy's eyes but she smiled steadfastly, and after a searching look Melly responded, giving Cathy the odd sensation that all was forgiven.

Delight gave her a sparkling spontaneity which caught the

attention of everyone else in the room. She knew most of them so it was not difficult to pick up where she had left off two years before, but her pleasure faded almost immediately as she felt the impact of Emma Theobald's sullen, furious glare. Glowering moodily into his glass, Peter stood beside but not touching her, resentment an almost palpable aura about him.

Melly said firmly, 'Of course I don't have to introduce you to Emma and Peter, but this is Emma's brother, Jake Ferrers, who flew in late last night.'

Cathy's eyes flew to meet Peter's flat, angry stare. Danger prickled down her nerve-ends, intensified as Emma sent her a tight, vindictive smile.

'But we've met.' It was a drawl, lightly laced with innuendo. 'Unfortunately we didn't get to exchange names.'

It was the man who knew so much about the first emperor of China.

Melly looked from one to the other, her dark eyes a little speculative, but her voice was mild as she said, 'Jake, this is Cathy Durrant. She's just arrived back in New Zealand after a couple of years spent roaming.'

From beneath drooping lashes Cathy watched as he acknowledged the faint warning note in Melly's voice with a wry, totally worldly lift of his black brows. Shock at his appearance had snatched words from her mouth; she could only extend her hand in a gesture as automatic as it was reluctant.

It was taken, and for the second time within ten minutes kissed. But this time her cool skin heated beneath the firm male lips which lingered on it and she had to fight an impulse to pull away.

He must have felt her tension, but he took his time about releasing her hand, and when at last he did Cathy was visited by a crazy premonition that he had staked some sort of claim. Poor Peter, she thought dizzily. He was no competition for this man, with his virile authority and inbuilt knowledge of women.

In a husky little voice she said the first thing that came into her mind. 'How long are you planning to stay, Mr Ferrers?'

'Longer than I expected.'

What did that mean? Without volition she looked up to be caught in the snare of turquoise eyes, bold and speculative and appreciative all at once. Experienced, her brain warned her. This man knew exactly what he was doing, and for some reason he wanted to keep her off balance.

Very coolly she smiled and stepped back, bringing Melly back into the conversation. It was done with charm but it was a rebuff and she was satisfied that he knew it when those astonishing eyes narrowed slightly.

Emma's voice was an odd compound of shrillness and pride as she moved to stand beside her brother. Possessively she said, 'Ever since I got married Jake has been promising to come to see me, and now he's finally here!'

Staking a claim, Cathy thought. Poor Emma. But couldn't she see what her open adoration of her brother was doing to Peter's self-respect? Her eyes flicked across to Peter; he lifted his glass in a tiny mute salute and tipped the rest of his drink down his throat as though it was what he had been waiting for all evening.

Poor Peter.

Jake Ferrers had watched the silent little by-play but there was no expression in the strongly carved sculpture of his face, neither condemnation nor contempt. He smiled down at his sister, and as though it had been a message she said quickly, 'Oh, there's someone I must say hello to. I'll see you later, Cathy. Come on, Peter.'

The words sounded quick and forced and she swung away quickly as if afraid that Cathy might see something in her expression. Melly, too, made her excuses. Cathy said nothing, watching as Emma snapped a single sentence at Peter, words that brought an instant's hectic colour to his face. Without a word he swung on his heel and headed across to the sideboard to pour himself another drink, leaving his wife abandoned in the middle of the room.

Cathy's teeth savaged her bottom lip; she nerved herself to go over to Emma. A hand on her arm stopped her.

'I doubt,' Jake Ferrers drawled, 'that you would be very welcome.'

'You go, then.'

'Or I,' he said aloofly.

But Emma was no longer alone. Ever an excellent hostess, Melly gathered her up to meet another young matron, not betraying by look or word that she had seen the whole unpleasant little incident.

Cathy's dark brows unpleated themselves although the eyes she turned on Jake Ferrers were still shadowed. Broad shoulders moved in a shrug. 'All marriages have sticky patches,' he said casually. 'They'll get over it.'

She almost opened her mouth to point out with asperity that if Emma continued to measure her husband against her brother and find him wanting, she might not get the chance to get over it, but thought better of it. After all, he would naturally take his sister's side. And it was really no business of either of them.

So she said, 'Yes, of course.'

And found herself in the unusual situation of not knowing what to say next. Very bright, almost blazing, his eyes were fixed on the soft contours of her mouth, and she felt the tension in him with every nerve. The muscles in her throat moved nervously as she swallowed; he watched that too, as though fascinated, and when his long hand lifted to touch the lock of bright hair that clung to her throat it was like a charge of electricity through her body.

'Nobody told me how beautiful you were,' he said softly.

CHAPTER TWO

THE buzz of conversation faded into nothingness. Cathy couldn't have spoken if she had tried, and, sensibly, she didn't try. Instead, wide and bewildered, her eyes clung to his, searching for the same unbidden response in the tough uncompromising face bent towards her. What she found, a kind of savage hunger in the impact of that brilliant gaze, made her take a nervous step backwards, breaking the spell. His hand dropped to his side.

Voices impinged, she heard someone laugh, and as she watched, the feverish glitter in his eyes was extinguished by a bleak barrier as though he was superimposing a wall of restraint over whatever emotions had created that moment of truth.

In a stranger's drowsy voice she said, 'I—thank you.'

'Like a dream,' he said, but there was something almost impersonal in the way his eyes scanned the length of her body. 'Small, yet voluptuous, as vivid as a flame.'

Colour scorched along the fine fair skin which went with her bright hair. Embarrassed and oddly hurt by his appraisal, she drew herself up to her inconsiderable height, retorting with some asperity, 'Thank you again—I think.'

His mouth widened in a wicked, understanding grin. 'All I did was touch you,' he said softly. 'What do you think might happen when I kiss you?'

When, not *if*, she noticed. Her first impulse was to deny the shattering effect he had on her but she was not stupid. He knew what had happened. However, sheer self-defence made her say sweetly, 'I don't know that I'd care to try it. I'm a firm believer in controlling my own life.'

23

'And you don't think you could control yourself if I kissed you?'

'Oh, I trust myself implicitly,' she parried smartly.

An eyebrow lifted in mocking scrutiny. 'But not me? How can I reassure you? I'm not turned on by force. Are you?'

She shivered, remembering some of the sights she had seen in that small corner of the jungle. 'No!'

'On the other hand,' he said outrageously, 'I could well be turned on if you tried to force me.'

Cathy couldn't prevent the giggle bubbling through her lips. He had to be a couple of inches over six feet, a foot taller than she was, and all of it was leanly elegant predation. She said kindly, 'You don't need to worry, I'd be exceptionally gentle,' and then blushed with horror at her runaway tongue.

Fortunately, because although there was amusement it was untempered by mercy in the gaze locked on to hers, they were interrupted. Emma almost pushed in between them, her pretty, petulant face rigid with anger as she said to Cathy, 'You mustn't monopolise Jake, you know, there are lots of other people who want to meet him tonight.'

It was the tone rather than the words which Cathy found so offensive. Her first instinct was to retaliate, but something in the pale blue eyes stopped the acid words before they left her tongue. Emma gave a strange little smirk, but she couldn't hide the unhappiness in her expression. Cathy shrugged, and smiled, and said abruptly, 'Of course.'

Absorbed in thought she allowed herself to be snared by a friend of her mother's, and spent the next few minutes listening with every appearance of interest to a stream of vapid conversation which she could answer without concentrating.

She had been so angry with Emma's treatment of Peter that she had fallen into the oldest trap of all, that of viewing the situation from only one angle. But Emma was suffering too. Perhaps her behaviour was a symptom of some deeper pain.

'Really?' she murmured absently, her eyes drifting around

the room, avoiding only that part of it occupied by Emma and her brother and a couple of women who were flirting with him.

Peter was standing by the bar, his handsome face drawn and defiant as he helped himself to yet another drink. Smiling sweetly at the woman beside her, Cathy waited for the next small silence before she made an excuse and slipped across the room to stand beside him, her small slender hand gripping his wrist.

'You've had enough,' she whispered with a total lack of tact.

His brows came together but he did not resist as she twisted the glass from his hand and put it on a convenient table.

Then he said wearily, 'Cathy, I love you. Why didn't I marry you?'

She could have said a multitude of things, passed it off with a joke, but something in his eyes convinced her that he really thought he was speaking the truth. The last thing she wanted to do was hurt him more than he was already hurting, so she hesitated, searching for the words, and then his expression changed and he forced a comparatively cheerful smile to his face.

'Hello, Jake. Got over your jet-lag? Do you know, Cath, this iron man actually admitted to a slight touch of tiredness this morning! And after flying only half-way round the world!'

Jake couldn't have heard Peter's despairing query because his expression was bland, almost uninterested. Cathy repressed a hissing sigh of relief, only to hear her voice gabbling as she pitched in with a story of jet-lag until the sound of her high-pitched, almost breathless words shocked her into silence. Her skin felt strange, she thought wonderingly. As though it had been burned; sensitive, almost tender. And when Jake Ferrers took her glass from her she flinched away, because his fingers lingered against hers in a caress as deliberate as it was fleeting.

Why this man? The situation was difficult enough without the added complication of this incandescent physical response to a man she didn't even know!

For the rest of the evening Cathy was haunted by an unsettling premonition of disaster. Somehow she managed to cope with the burden of Jake Ferrers' attention but she began to feel a little as a stalked animal must feel, the constant, impalpable sense of danger whipping up the adrenalin in her bloodstream so that she became almost feverish with excitement. He sat beside her at dinner and, although both were meticulous in fulfilling their social obligations, each time their eyes met it gave rise to a suffocating blankness in Cathy's brain.

She was not even surprised when hours later she found herself in his Jaguar giving directions to her apartment, although her sense of self-preservation kept her tense, her small figure rigid against the leather upholstery as he drove skilfully through the darkened streets. Emma had said nothing when she realised what was happening, but her expression had been only too easy to read. Cathy wondered worriedly if there was something pathological in the other woman's dislike of her. Unless Emma felt like that about any woman who caught Jake's eye.

So lost in thought was she that his observation made her jump. 'You seem,' he drawled, 'to be on very good terms with your ex-husband and his wife.'

Hauteur chilled her tones almost to ice. 'Why not?'

His teeth showed momentarily. 'Oh, why not indeed? Much the best way to go about things, all modern and sophisticated. Are you very sophisticated, Cathy?'

Somehow, because it had sounded like a direct attack, she contrived to overlay the raggedness in her voice with a lazy boredom. 'I like to think so.'

As if satisfied, he made no reply, and within minutes they reached the street outside her apartment block. After he had eased the big car into the kerb he switched off the engine and got out. Cathy watched him carefully, correctly assessing the lithe grace with which he walked around the front of the car. He was in perfect physical condition, a natural athlete honed to the peak.

A trickle of sensation slithered the length of her backbone. Excitement? Or fear? She didn't know, but every warning instinct lying dormant in her subconscious was throbbing into life.

She accepted his company up the steps but after he had unlocked the door she made no effort to go in, turning her face up to say evenly, 'You don't have to come any further. The building has good security.'

He smiled, eyes gleaming beneath heavy lids. 'If I promise not to seduce you, will you give me a cup of coffee?' And before she could do more than begin to shake her head he went on persuasively, 'I want to talk to you about Emma and Peter.'

Her gaze sharpened. She searched his face, realising with a shock that it was totally impassive, giving nothing away. The autocratic features spoke of concentrated authority, the straight mouth was controlled, and what went on in the finely shaped dark head was beyond understanding. After a long moment she inclined her head gravely and led the way to the lift.

But once in the sitting-room he looked around with that unreadable expression and asked, 'Your choice of furnishings?'

Startled, she followed his appraisal. 'No, I lease it furnished. Why?'

'It's eighties chic, the same the world over. You look like a tiger cub stranded in a flower garden.'

Astonishment made her laugh. 'Looks can be deceptive.'

'Sometimes. Several people tried to describe you to me but none of them came anywhere near the full impact. They all said that you were beautiful, in a seductive, passionate way, vivid and exotic and spoiled. They were right, but not entirely. The reality is much more stunning.'

The words sounded—fulsome, almost calculating, as though he was testing her. She raised her brows and looked him coolly in the face, letting her expression show what she thought of his praise.

'Not impressed by flattery?' He seemed amused, wicked laughter gleaming beneath his lashes.

Her shoulders moved in a tiny shrug. 'I know how I look,' she said flatly. 'I conform to a certain type of feminine pulchritude which is fashionable at this moment. A hundred years ago I'd have been thought a very odd-looking woman. Your sister is more classically good-looking.'

'Emma hasn't half of what you have, and you know it,' he told her. 'Your colouring is outstanding, but it's what lies behind both features and colouring that catches the eye.'

She looked puzzled, wondering what on earth he was talking about. He smiled, a lazy, sensual appreciation, and lifted a hand to outline with a gentle finger the full curves of her mouth. Her chest lifted in a swift intake of breath. She could smell a faint, teasing aroma of male, aphrodisiac and arousing. Something strange happened to her bones and she almost gasped at the stab of raw sensation that pierced the pit of her stomach. Her head tilted; she looked from half-closed eyes up into a face suddenly lean and feral, intent upon conquest.

'Yes,' he said softly, 'this is what men see when they look at you. A sulky mouth that promises all sorts of delicious excesses, eyes to lose one's soul in, and the intangible, potent aura of experience. You know it all, sweetheart, and you know just what effect that has on men.'

If she hadn't been so seduced by the deep note of desire throbbing beneath the words and the strange ache they roused all through her body she might have laughed. Experienced! If only he knew! As it was, something must have shown in the smoky blue of her eyes because his mouth curled into a knowing smile, hard and suddenly grim as death.

'You like it, don't you,' he said. 'It gives you power over men and women, that animal attraction. Is that why you won't leave poor Theobald alone to work through his marriage woes?'

Her head jerked. Sudden flames kindled in her gaze as she said angrily, 'I have nothing to do with his marriage!'

'No?' He didn't believe her, that was plain, yet there was a kind of understanding in his face as he looked down at her. 'You're not just a little bit in love with him?'

'No.' She was going to tell him more when he interrupted.

'In that case, how about relieving my poor, silly sister's mind by pretending to fall in love with me?'

She whirled away, her mind a bewildering compound of sheer rage at having been tricked, and a familiar grief at being rejected. Why on earth should she have thought that he was as attracted to her as she was to him? Hadn't she been shown, time and time again, that those she loved couldn't love her back? Her mother, her grandfather, Trent . . . A dreary little list!

Sheer pride lifted her glowing head. She said carefully, 'I think not. It wouldn't do any good. You must have noticed tonight that Emma doesn't like it when you pay attention to me.'

'Emma is as jealous as hell. Wouldn't you be, when you're continually compared to a woman who looks as you do?'

She opened her mouth to protest, met the cold lance of his scrutiny, and closed it again, frowning. Surely he was wrong? And yet, she had only had heard Peter's side of things.

But she was not going to put herself in jeopardy by pretending to fall in love with this man. She knew his sort, even if Emma had not made any bones about the very physical nature of his relationships with women. A bitter little smile curved her mouth. Wouldn't he get a shock if he discovered that the woman he thought a sensual witch was still a virgin!

Aloud, her voice robbed of the intimate laughing note which made it so beguiling, she said, 'I don't believe you. Peter and I grew up together. He doesn't think of me like that. He married your sister, not me.'

'How does he think of you?'

Anger edged her voice as she turned to confront him. He had not moved, yet somehow he seemed to loom, menacing and predatory, a darkly dangerous presence in the lovely, impersonal room. 'We are *friends.*' She stressed the word with a savage little snap. 'I don't want to have anything to do with—with——'

'With me?' he supplied blandly. 'What do I lack that the other men in your life have?'

'Nothing.' And that was the truth. The only other man in her life had been Trent; a very hard act to follow. In fact, Jake was the only man she had met since her divorce who didn't seem pale and juiceless beside Trent. Breathlessly, she went on, 'It wouldn't be good idea, Jake. I'm sorry for Emma—and for Pete—but there's nothing we can do for them. They are going to have to work this through themselves.'

'And you refuse to help.' The words were spoken without inflection, but there was something in the cast of his features which made her shiver.

Her teeth came down for a painful moment on her bottom lip. He was profoundly disturbing, his very stillness a threat. For a crazy moment she wondered whether she should agree to his wild plan, but he was too compelling, too much of a danger to her peace of mind. Only fools set themselves up for pain.

So she shook her head and said very firmly, 'I refuse to interfere.'

'Even if I appeal to your better nature?'

'I'm sorry?'

He paused, then said calmly, 'Emma is not the most stable of women. Our parents had the sort of marriage where the image is everything, the reality nothing, but both were devoted to her. As I was. When she was twelve they left her while they went on a cruise. They died in a fire on the liner.'

Cathy's eyes softened, but she couldn't rid herself of the feeling that he was manipulating her. 'I'm sorry,' seemed inadequate, but she said it anyway.

He shrugged. 'Emma took it very badly. She became very insecure, and needed a considerable amount of help to overcome it. However, she managed. Then she met Peter. And fell in love with him.'

'Which did not please you,' she said shrewdly.

Wide shoulders moved in another, smaller shrug. 'No. I thought he was lightweight, not the sort of man to give Emma the stability she should have, but it seemed that he was what she wanted, possibly what she needs, someone who is basically kind and easy-going. And she was determined to have him. She has always known what she wants.'

She nodded, and waited.

'And for years she has been perfectly all right. A little neurotic, perhaps, but no more so than many women who lead normal lives. However, when she married him she hadn't realised there was another woman in Peter's life.' He cut her automatic objection off short, saying impatiently, 'I presume that when you went off to look around the world Peter decided that he was no longer bound, and so free to fall in love with Emma. But you came back.'

She said slowly, 'Wait a minute. You think Pete is my lover?'

'What I think is not important. I don't give a damn except as it affects Emma, and she thinks that if you're not lovers now you were, and you could well be again.' The deep uninflected voice paused again, then went smoothly on, 'You must admit that he's spent a couple of nights with you since you came back.'

Cathy's temper was being ridden on a short rein, but she managed to keep some control. 'If she stopped comparing Peter—to his detriment—with you, he might not get so angry that he comes looking for someone who understands him.'

'Don't give me that rubbish!'

She said curtly, 'You started this, not me. I've known Pete

since I was born, and he is not happy!'

'And not likely to be as long as you are hovering on the edge of their marriage, offering sympathy and comfort! If you'd leave them alone to work out their own affairs——'

She couldn't help it. She laughed scornfully. 'Why don't you?'

She had scored because he seemed to hesitate, as though her direct attack had surprised him. Then he said slowly, 'I'm not stupid enough to think that anything I can do will help. But I can at least see that those on the periphery realise what they are doing. However unwisely Emma is behaving, she believes you to be a real threat to her marriage. Frightened people are rarely sensible, but now that I've met you—and heard a little about you and your family—I think her instincts could well be right.'

The reference to her grandfather made her bite her lip. She said wearily, 'I'm sorry for Emma, because if she keeps on behaving in this neurotic way she's going to lose Pete. She blames me, but that's not how Peter sees it.'

Something dark and frightening flickered in the jewelled depths of his eyes. She lifted her chin, finishing quickly, 'Anyway, I'm not going to be here much longer.'

'Why?'

'That's not any of your business. But I'm leaving Auckland in a couple of days, and I won't be back for several months.'

He was watching her as if measuring the truth of her statement, a probing, glinting assessment which brought defiant colour into her cheeks. An instinctive fear crawled like a loathsome insect across her skin, pulling it tight. Yet his face was immobile. Only his eyes moved, from imprisoning her gaze to search out the pulse which throbbed in her pale throat, and then back to the soft line of her mouth. It was intimidation, pure and simple and devastating, and he was doing it without uttering a word.

She almost winced, and his expression relaxed. She could read amusement there, but it was mixed with mockery, and both were chilling.

'Perhaps that's all that's necessary,' he drawled, and turned and left.

She locked the door behind him, almost shaking with tension.

She set off for the bach the next day, riding the ferry past the many islands of the Gulf, serene and beautiful beneath the spring sun like uncut gems embedded in a sheet of silver. Slowly the restless hours she had spent after Jake's departure began to fade. Her strong will pushed the memories of the night before to the back of her mind until she relaxed, allowing herself to surrender once more to childhood's uncomplicated delight in the moment. Deep inside her something tight and hard began to unwind.

At Waiheke she disembarked to catch the waiting taxi. When her grandfather was alive they had travelled to their island on his big cruiser or in a helicopter, sometimes in the little amphibian which served the islands in the Gulf. Those days were gone. The cruiser had been sold after his death and the helicopter was used by the executives of the conglomerate, now ruled by Trent. Motuiti, the little island, dreamed on with only the Stallworthys, a married couple who had been the resident caretakers there for at least twenty years, to keep it company.

As the taxi took her the length of Waiheke, island of ebbing water to the Maoris, Cathy smiled, because coming here was exactly what she needed. First of all she would laze, unwind from the past two years, and then she would think about redecorating the bach. The whole summer would slip through her fingers, every long golden day and warm blue night savoured like a rare and precious delicacy.

She refused to admit that she was running away from Jake Ferrers.

Only a few hours ago. Peter had rung from work, angry because Emma had 'had another tantrum, because,' he said bitterly, 'her beloved brother took off with you! You may not have realised it, but Emma is possessive of everyone she owns!'

'Well, she won't have to worry any more. I'm going across to the island today.'

He sighed. 'Wish I could come with you. I tell you, between her and Jake, I am not looking forward to this Christmas.'

'Is he staying that long?'

'Yep. Apparently he's going to write another book, or play, or something. Anyway, he's going to find a place to live and bash out another bestseller. Emma is thrilled, of course. He gives her much more status than her husband does!'

Tartly Cathy retorted, 'Perhaps if her husband didn't wallow in self-pity and kept off the booze she might feel she got some status from him too.'

'Ouch! Don't you turn on me too, Cath! You're the only person I get any sympathy from!'

Slowly, feeling the way, she said quietly, 'Perhaps you shouldn't ask for sympathy, Pete. I——'

'Just what the hell did Jake tell you last night? Did he try to fill you full——'

She interrupted in her turn. 'Pete, naturally he's worried, but believe me, we discussed your marriage only in the most general of terms and we did not even mention blame! Emma is his sister, he's fond of her and of course he wants her to be happy.'

'And he,' Peter said deliberately, 'is a bastard of the first order when it comes to women. Believe that, if you believe nothing else of the man. Oh, yes, I saw the way he was looking at you last night, as if you were a delicious little morsel for him to snap up. He loves women, but he's got no staying power. When he gets sick of one he moves on without a qualm. I helped you pick up the pieces after that fiasco of a marriage of yours; I don't ever want to see you go through that anguish again. Jake Ferrers is a dangerous man, Cathy.'

In a subdued voice she said, 'I know, but I'm not going to

be around to see anything of him, so whether he's dangerous or not isn't going to make any difference to me! And he does love his sister! Couldn't you confide in him?'

'Are you crazy? He doesn't give a damn about me!'

'Peter, do you love Emma?'

Heavily, after a tense moment, he said, 'Yes. With all my heart. Ironic, isn't it. Because I don't think she loves me at all.'

'Oh, Pete,' she whispered.

'Well, it happens.' She could almost see the effort it took him to infuse a flippant note into his voice. 'You know it happens, Cathy darling. Anyway, enjoy yourself on the island. Remember the fun we used to have as kids there? Have another summer like that for me, there's a good girl.'

Now, standing on the jetty opposite her island, Cathy watched the taxi grumble its way up the hill and thought with a touch of wistfulness that during those long-ago holidays there had always been family and friends. Now, both she and Peter were very much alone. In a way she had always been alone.

She leaned against the rail to look down into the water. The sun beat down on her unprotected head, kindling the heavy mass of her hair to flames. With half-closed eyes she listened to the faint lapping of the water against the biscuit-coloured sand, the curious query of a blackbacked gull as it strutted at the other end of the jetty. Beneath her in the water galaxies of tiny fish clustered and darted in perfect unison, now colourless, now flashing silver in the sunlight, quite unaware of the existence of anything more important than their own small beings.

From the corner of her eye she could see the locked shed where the island Land Rover kept company with the caretakers' car. She smiled, wondering how Mr and Mrs Stallworthy were. Well, she would soon see, because from across the water the sound of the outboard motor provided a drowsy but rapidly increasing counterpoint to the call of the gulls.

Cathy looked beyond the small runabout to the familiar outline of the hills of the island. Heat and light beat down on her small face, picking out the definite lines of jaw and cheek, the ripe readiness of her mouth, the seductive curve of long dark lashes. As the runabout approached the jetty she shook her head to clear the dazzle from her eyes. The sun danced in the tumbled tresses, flame and gold and bronze blended in passionate disorder.

At that moment Cathy was perfectly happy.

The engine cut; she widened her eyes to look into the mocking face of Jake Ferrers. Her heart seemed to leap through her ribs.

Inanely she asked, 'Where is Mr Stallworthy?'

'In hospital.' He looped the rope over one of the piles and swung on to the jetty to bend to pick up her case, the muscles in those long legs suddenly outlined beneath the faded blue denim.

'Wait a minute.' Unconscious arrogance sharpened her tone. 'Why are you here?'

He dumped her case into the runabout and turned to face her. 'Because, madam,' he said softly, 'someone had to be here to convey your precious little self across to the island. In the absence of the caretakers, I volunteered.'

She bit her lip but insisted, 'How did you know—what's the matter with Mr Stallworthy?'

'Appendicitis,' he said succinctly. The box of groceries followed her case.

Cathy dragged her eyes away from the corded strength of his tanned arms to demand curtly, 'Why are you here?'

'I happened to be talking to your ex-husband when Mrs Stallworthy rang him. Her husband was in agony but she didn't know what to do because you were arriving today. Addison organised a helicopter in no time flat and I came out on it to meet you.'

'What were you doing with Trent?' His ironic brows made

her realise how rude she was. Heat singed her cheeks and she
continued hastily, 'I'm sorry, that's none of my business.
Thank you for meeting me. I assume you're taking the Land
Rover back to the ferry. When you get back to the wharf, park
it at the nearest garage; they'll look after it until someone can
pick it up.'

'What assumptions you make,' he taunted smoothly. 'No,
I'm coming back with you. I promised Mrs Stallworthy I'd
feed her hens and milk the cow.'

'Oh.' She didn't know what to do. How long did he plan to
stay? She could feed the hens, but she had never milked a cow
in her life. He grinned, those crystalline eyes knowing and
amused, and waited as she hesitated on the warm planks of the
jetty, her small body tautly expressing both her irresolution
and her resentment.

After a moment which seemed to stretch for ever he
banished the air of patient resignation he had assumed and
commanded, 'Hop in.'

Weakly she obeyed, sitting very still and staring towards the
steadily enlarging island as her mind worked furiously. What
on earth did he plan to do? Cows were milked twice a day. Did
he plan to stay the night? Her unseeing eyes fell to her hands,
prim and still in her lap. Deep within her rigid body a
forbidden excitement began to fizz through her blood. The
sun sparkled on the sea in myriad silver points of light; she was
chagrined to realise that her feelings reflected the ocean,
buoyant and hopeful and glittery.

She asked again, 'How is Mr Stallworthy? Do you know?'

'Not yet, his wife is going to ring when the hospital gives
some indication, but I told her to stay there until he came out.'

Just like that, as though it was his business! Cathy darted a
resentful look towards him, saw in a fleeting second the way
his eyes were narrowed against the glare. A small taunting
smile pulled at the corners of his mouth. Clearly he was
waiting for her to point out that he had no right to make any

promises to the Stallworthys.

Demurely she murmured, 'Thank you.'

Had she surprised him? Although his expression revealed nothing she rather thought that somewhere behind the angular mask of bone and bronzed skin he was surprised. However, if he was he made a quick recovery.

'My pleasure,' he said, annoyingly cheerful.

She turned her head to look back over the bow, pushing back the hair that whipped across her face. Her fingers threaded through the heavy silk in a gesture she would have been surprised to know was provocative, presenting to his sardonic scrutiny her glossy well defined profile with its sultry mouth and seductively drooping eyelids and tough, determined little chin.

She didn't see his eyes harden into chips of light because her attention was wholly on the bay coming into view around a low headland. A reef ran out to one side, protecting the white sand from any easterlies. Two or three hundred yards out to sea was a low island covered in gnarled old pohutukawa trees. More rocks filled in the gap between the island and the headland, so that the only way to take a vessel into the cove was through a narrow but deep channel that wound among them.

On the bank above the cove, set back so that its walls were barely visible above the sheltering trees, was the bach, a sprawling old wooden farmhouse set in a grove of more trees. Grassy hills rose steeply behind and the sun gleamed invitingly on a pane of glass in one of the big windows; a surge of emotion closed her throat.

Jake took the runabout through the reef as expertly as no doubt he did everything else. Firmly repressing the images that supposition conjured up Cathy slipped off her shoes and flung them up the beach in the childish ritual which had always marked the beginning of each holiday, waiting until the boat nosed into the soft, wet sand before she jumped lithely over. The engine cut; the sudden silence seemed to shout at them. She winced at the chilly water but held out a hand for the groceries.

'I'll bring them,' he said curtly. 'You go on up.'

Well, he was certainly stronger than she was. Cathy nodded and took her first steps into the sunwarmed sand, her toes sinking luxuriously into the powdery depths.

Why had he suddenly turned snappy? Deciding to ignore him and his moods, she turned haughtily away and walked up the path to the house with a straight back and head held so high that her shoulders felt the strain. Beneath the great sweeping branches of the pohutukawas the grass was thick and springy, mown kikuyu, the scent of it as familiar as childhood, as evocative as an antique wedding-gown. Hibiscus and oleander bushes were clustered by the house, gearing up for the summer show of pinks and golds. Across the lawn was the wide stone terrace, and there were the french doors, open.

Cathy swallowed hard. The last time she had been here her grandmother had still been alive. It seemed impossible that she would never again watch the small fragile figure walk out across the terrace and bend to pick some flower, holding it tenderly between fingers twisted by age.

But death was inevitable. Cathy's skin paled as she remembered some of the things she had seen in the jungle. At least her grandmother hadn't suffered torture and starvation and bitter, bitter grief before death came as the only friend she had left.

She stood in the middle of the big cheerfully shabby sitting-room and looked around, her eyes wide and shadowy in her small face. To the man who came in behind her she seemed like a forlorn doll. But the moment she felt his presence the *triste* expression vanished, replaced by determination and a caution that made her look older and harder.

Without speaking he deposited her case on the floor and went out in the direction of the kitchen.

He certainly seemed to know his way around, she thought, subduing with a healthy dose of resentment the excitement licking in slow flames through her body. She followed him, brows drawing together as she watched him deftly remove the groceries from the carton and arrange them on the bench.

'Why have you taken it on yourself to milk Mrs Stallworthy's cow?'

Even to herself the question sounded ridiculous, and he cast her a quick contemptuous glance, reacting to the demand in her tone rather than the words.

'Because I want to,' he said calmly.

She shook her head in frustration. 'You can't just stay here! I don't want you to.'

'I'm not your guest.' He was mocking her, his eyes very bright and piercing as they scanned her flushed face. 'I'm afraid that for once in your life, my dear, what you want is not vitally important. After all, you sure as hell can't milk a cow!'

She couldn't help her laughter. And the astonishment in his face made her amusement even more impossible to resist. After a moment the cynicism faded from his features to be replaced by humour; she realised, with a kind of breathless wonder, that when he laughed he was the most gorgeous man she had ever seen.

When she had regained control she pointed out gravely, 'This cow seems to be assuming great importance in my life. Will you teach me how to milk her?'

'So that you can send me on my way? Never.' The amusement faded; he was watching her with a gleam in his eye which made her heart begin to pick up speed. 'It is a little difficult to imagine the spoilt, sophisticated Cathy Durrant milking a cow.'

Her mouth twisted in a wry smile as she recalled a few of the things she had done in the past years. 'Really?' she said, copying her grandmother's politely dismissive note. 'Tell me, where do you plan to stay until Mrs Stallworthy comes back?'

Something like scorn gave an ugly line to his lips but it vanished so quickly she thought she must have misread it. He answered coolly, 'At the cottage.'

An uncompromisingly stark answer, one that brought a mutinous expression to her face. She began to object, then looked at him, over six feet of lean muscle and strength, not bothering to hide a definite anticipatory glitter in his eyes, and decided to remain silent. It was no use batting her head against a stone wall. But she was damned if he was going to make himself wholly at home.

Possibly he was so arrogantly confident of his masculine attractions that he anticipated a pleasant holiday affair. Firmly repressing any memory of that strange fiery attraction which had flared between them, she decided defiantly that if that was so he would soon find out that the spoilt Miss Cathy Durrant didn't go in for bedroom games!

It never occurred to her that he might have rape on his mind. Some feminine instinct, one buried so deeply she wasn't even aware she possessed it, was satisfied that the danger he represented had nothing to do with that sort of brutality. And it certainly didn't occur to her to wonder why she was so confident that she could control the situation.

CHAPTER THREE

AS IF he could read the thoughts racing around her brain, Jake smiled, not very pleasantly, and dumped the empty carton out through the back door. 'I'll burn it later,' he said before calmly walking off through the house.

When Cathy caught him up he had her case in his hand and was on his way to the passage which led to the bedrooms.

'I can take that,' she blurted.

He lifted his brows at her but didn't pause. In a manner she had to admit was totally undignified she was forced to trail along behind him as he set off towards the room which had always been her grandparents'.

'Not there,' she said hastily. 'This is my room.'

It was big, decorated the way a decorator had thought suitable for a teenager, all ruffles and embroidery with an antique half-tester bed. Cathy had never liked it, but had endured it because her grandmother had had it done for her fifteenth birthday; for some reason the sight of him dominating the pretty, clichéd room made her hackles rise.

'Thank you,' she said. Dismissal rang coldly in her voice, showed in her face. Later she was to try to convince herself that it was habit born of her years overseas which took her hand to her bag. She had twisted open the purse before she found her fingers imprisoned in a cruel grip.

Already mortified at her crassness, she still lifted her head proudly. The vivid aquamarine gaze burned into her face but all he said was, 'This is New Zealand, Cathy. No tipping, remember?'

Before she could stammer out a reply the fierce anger was transmuted into something just as deadly. 'Not money, any-

42

way,' he murmured, and bent his head to hers. He made himself master of the sudden leaping response she couldn't hide.

The kiss was a far from subtle punishment meant to put her firmly in her place. But worse than his casual lust was her febrile reaction, the swift, merciless singing in her blood which almost made her forget caution.

She managed to draw a fast, impeded breath. One hand curled into a small but serviceable fist and she punched with every ounce of strength into his solar plexus.

He must have sensed her intention, for he had time to tighten the hard muscles across his midriff, but even so his breath exhaled like a small explosion into her mouth. He straightened and his other hand flashed to grip hers; her eyes blazed defiant blue as he pinned her fist against the taut shield of his chest. He was smiling, but there was no humour in the reckless face bent to hers. For a tense moment they stood like bitter lovers, so close that the thud of his heart seemed to reverberate up through her arm to her brain, blotting out all thought; yet even with the taste of him seducing her mouth and the sight of him filling her eyes she gave not an inch, small and indomitable.

Then, beneath her imprisoned fingers she felt the strong muscles relax as, incredibly, he laughed. 'My mistake,' he said, and lifted her hand to his mouth.

Again he astonished her. She expected a kiss but with eyes still narrowed and fixed almost blindly on her face he bit gently at the base of her thumb. It gave her an odd, thrillingly erotic sensation. Cathy shivered, trying to repress the tiny electric shocks which ran through her body. Then the heated pressure lifted, the tingling graze of his teeth relaxed, and she was free. She stepped back, struggling to regain some poise, only to betray just how she had been affected by childishly rubbing her hand against her thigh in a vain effort to wipe away the sensation.

Yet her voice was firm, almost imperious as she said, 'I don't like being mauled by strangers.'

He grinned. 'A very proper attitude. But would you say that we're strangers? Almost family, I'd have thought. After all, my sister is married to your childhood playmate. We must be related, in some way.'

And who, she thought robustly, are you trying to fool? Looking up into the hard hunter's face above her she was suddenly visited by a premonition of peril so acute that she shivered. Aimlessly she looked around, saying vaguely, 'Oh, hardly.'

Anything to break the primitive spell of his masculinity.

'Although,' the deep, amused voice continued, 'I don't see you as a sister, exactly.'

'No. No,' she repeated more strongly. She swallowed, desperate to get him out of the room before something happened, before the peril he represented caught her in a trap of sensuality. 'Nor I you as a brother. The local bully, perhaps.'

A second's electric silence, then, 'And what exactly do you mean by that?'

'I don't need you here. But I can't throw you out.'

He didn't like that. The angular lines of his face tightened, eclipsing all mockery. Very curtly he said, 'Mrs Stallworthy felt that she could not leave you here alone. She was all set to struggle back and forth by ferry and taxi until her husband recovers. I managed to convince her that I would look after your precious little person so that she would feel happier about staying over in town. And as neither she nor your ex-husband seemed confident that you would do the sensible thing and go back to Auckland, that meant staying here with you. I don't really care whether you like the idea or not.'

With a sweetness that dripped sarcasm she retaliated, 'I'm so sorry. Perhaps it's just that the little I've heard about you didn't give me the impression that you indulged in altruism.'

He surveyed her, his narrow black brows drawn together, the sea-coloured eyes chips of ice. Cathy didn't even lift her chin but her vivid face was set in lines as cold and hard, all the seductive loveliness transmuted into a will every bit as strong as her grandfather's.

Something dangerous and wild flicked behind his lashes, then he swung away, leaving her staring at him with dilated eyes. He walked with the lean powerful grace of a splendid male animal, all smooth, threatening force. Pictures sprang into her mind, images of a panther padding with feral grace across a desolate beautiful landscape, and she shivered again in the warm room.

When he had gone she put out a hand and touched one of a bowl of coneflowers, honey-golden on the table beside her bed. Her fingers stroked the stiff sepals; she thought fancifully that she could feel the slow tides of life through the cells, a counterpoint to the swiftness of the pulse that beat in her throat.

The sound of the telephone in the quiet house was a shocking intrusion but one that she welcomed. Curling up in the small chair by her bed she lifted the receiver, already aware of the identity of the caller.

'Settled in?' Peter asked jauntily after the usual preliminaries.

For some reason she didn't mention Jake's presence, merely giving a vague affirmative before asking, 'What do you want? Is anything wrong?'

He laughed, the false note increasing her uneasiness. 'Now, Cathy, why should anything be wrong? Except the usual, of course.'

'Oh Pete . . .'

'Ah, hell,' he said disgustedly. 'I know I shouldn't harass you like this. I suppose I want to be comforted.'

She tried again. 'What really happened last night?'

This time he didn't try to put her off. 'Another night,

another fight,' he said airily. 'But actually she's just rung me so that she could have another go. My work, of course, counts for nothing compared to the Shakespeare of the twentieth century. I'll bet she doesn't dare interrupt him when he's creating immortal literature. She rang specifically to tell me that she didn't like the way you and I spoke to each other last night. She doesn't want me herself, but she certainly doesn't want anyone else to be nice to me.'

'But that's not rational.'

'I've given up looking for threads of reason in Emma's brain patterns.'

Cathy stared sightlessly at the coneflowers. 'Pete, I'm so sorry, but I don't really think you should be discussing her with me.'

'There's no one else,' he said on a note of pain and loss. 'you're my safety-valve, Cathy. I felt so bloody alone before you came back home.'

Her heart melted. Tentatively she asked, 'Have you thought of counselling? Or perhaps—if you talked to Jake about her. He must know what she's like . . .'

He said savagely, 'Oh, he knows, he spelt it out to me when I dared propose. She needs love, and constant reassurance, she's never really got over her parents' death, she's a delicate little flower. He never said that she was unstable, but then, she's his sister, isn't she, and he's the personification of the protective male. What he didn't say, although he must know it, is that she's not above playing on her neuroses to manipulate people. Sometimes I wonder if she deliberately set up this situation so that he'd come and rescue her!'

'Oh, Pete!'

'She knows I love her, God knows, I've told her often enough, but apparently that's not enough. And although the whole world must do its utmost to support her fragile little psyche, apparently it doesn't apply the other way. It's perfectly all right for her to strip my confidence from me as fast as she can. My beloved wife is definitely strange,' he said, trying to hide the real pain in his voice with a show of belligerence. 'I think the problem is that she's always had Jake to run to, he's always been there to smooth her path, and she just can't cope without him to tell her what to do. So when she comes across a situation she doesn't know how to handle, she doesn't even try, she relapses into childish ways of dealing with her problems, throwing tantrums and crying. As soon as she realised that marriage wasn't the fairytale she thought it was going to be, she caved in and waited for him to ride in on his white horse and tidy everything up.'

Cathy nodded, her heart contracting. 'I suppose he was the one rock in her life after their parents died, and she's afraid of letting go, perhaps that he'll abandon her. Still, sooner or later she's going to have to learn to live without him. She can't go on clinging to him for security all her life. People grow away, they become immersed in their own interests.' She paused before offering a piece of hard-earned wisdom. 'In the end, the only person you can rely on is yourself.'

'I wouldn't mind, if only she showed some signs of trans-ferring some of that dependence to me,' he said wearily, following his own train of thought. 'But she hasn't.'

'Perhaps she feels that a husband who drinks too much or spends the night in another woman's house is not altogether trustworthy,' she suggested.

'Then she should ask herself why I left,' he snapped. 'We'd had such a fight—she was so bloody unreasonable I had to get away. Cathy, I was terrified I was going to hit her!'

'Pete!' He had blurted it out and she was truly horrified, but instinct warned her to treat it lightly. She said soothingly, 'Darling Pete, I know perfectly well that you wouldn't do it, that you *couldn't* do it. You know it, too.'

He said warmly, 'Cathy, I love you dearly. Thanks for listening. I really don't know what I'd do without you.'

She laughed, and purred in her most mock-seductive voice,

'Any time, darling, you know you can rely on me. I love you too.'

She hung up to the sound of his wry laughter and turned to meet the cold sea-green eyes of Jake Ferrers across the room. His face was a mask, bronze and sculptured, yet she gained a swift impression of extreme anger.

'What do you want?' she demanded, sharply because he frightened her.

Whatever strong emotion had caused that still menace was now under control. Apparently not at all put out by her rudeness he said smoothly, 'I came in to tell you that I'm going over to the cottage. There's quite a lot of work to be done there. I won't be back until dark.'

She frowned. 'Jake, it's really very kind of you to promise the Stallworthys you'd take over, but I can't let you do it. You're supposed to be on holiday! I'll get someone to——'

'Why bother?' He grinned. 'It will stop me from putting on weight.'

Involuntarily her eyes outlined the contours of his body. Not a spare ounce of flesh! She felt a tell-tale swathe of heat across her cheekbones and to draw attention away from the blush said hastily, 'What needs to be done?'

'Firewood to be cut, lawns to be mown, the vegetable garden to be weeded . . . Plenty. It looks as though your caretaker hasn't been feeling himself for some time.'

'Oh, poor Mr Stallworthy.' Well, if he wasn't going to mention it, she was. Her chin lifted a fraction as she said steadily, 'I was talking to Peter just then.'

His eyes narrowed a fraction but all he said was an unencouraging, 'So I heard.'

'It wasn't——' She hesitated, then said bluntly, afraid that her voice sounded a note of defiance, 'You may have misunderstood what I said.'

'Oh, I don't think so,' he drawled.

She tried again. 'We tease a lot. We understand each other,

Pete and I.'

'I'm sure you do,' he returned politely and walked off down the hall.

Not at all reassured, Cathy felt the smile fade from her face to leave her staring after him, a frown pulling her brows into a straight, thin line.

After a moment she shrugged and set herself to unpacking the few clothes she had brought, firmly repressing the vagrant, shameful thought that if she had known Jake Ferrers was going to be there she would have made sure she packed some rather more flattering things.

Muttering, she went into the bathroom. The shower helped. After it she paused in the passage outside the kitchen, her ears straining. Not a sound, apart from the call of a gull as it soared over the roof. It took only a few minutes to put together a salad of avocado and lettuce and tomato, but when it was done she hesitated a few seconds while deciding whether or not to call him; after a moment's thought she shrugged and with an air of defiance ate her share, resolutely repressing the realisation that her mouth still stung from that assult of a kiss.

Back in her bedroom she changed into a brief pair of shorts and a skimpy sun-top, wishing for possibly the thousandth time in her life that the genetic inheritance which had given her small bones and a slender waist had also seen to it that her breasts were in proportion, instead of being too voluptuous. An extra four inches on her legs would have been appreciated, too.

Outside the sun beckoned but she stood for a long time looking around her room, her expression pensive as she recalled the eighteen-year-old Cathy, so cruel in her aggressive self-centred adolescence, who had plotted in this very room to marry Trent.

Well, it had been a bitter lesson, but one well learned. Melly and Trent were idyllically happy now, and she had an interesting life mapped out for herself. And if she ever wondered whether one day there would be a love for her as strong as that which she saw whenever Trent looked at his wife, she hastened to push the thought away.

The terrace was empty of furniture so she went around the house to the big shed at the back which housed scuba gear and dinghies, all the extra gear necessary for the full enjoyment of a holiday at the beach. For a while, her expression wistful, she enjoyed herself poking around among the stuff stored there, but in a short time she found what she was looking for and picked up a redwood chair. After she had carried it to the terrace she struggled around with a lounger, positioning it carefully beneath the vine-hung pergola so that she could sprawl gracefully along it, looking out across the wide stretch of glittering sea to the mainland.

How often had she imagined herself back here? Uncounted times, and now the reality was spoilt by the presence of a man.

To keep his virile image at bay she allowed herself to worry about Peter's marriage. It was clear that Emma suffered from an overwhelming possessiveness as far as Jake was concerned. Was Peter right, did she feel that he could never live up to Jake's overwhelming standards?

Cathy's mouth tightened in an obstinate line. If that was so, she had a nerve! Peter probably never would compare favourably with his brother-in-law's formidable male assurance; few men would. Even though she didn't like him much Cathy had to admit that men who naturally, effortlessly captured attention with Jake's brand of sheer animal magnetism were few and far between. When that basic primitive attraction was coupled with an astounding talent and the disciplined, concentrated authority that Jake Ferrers wore like a second skin—well, poor Pete didn't have a show!

But he had plenty of other assets, not so obvious, not so immediately striking, but long-lasting and important. Like a genuinely kind heart, and the capacity to love selflessly; oh, Emma might think they counted for little beside her brother's peacock brilliance, but Cathy knew better.

A frown pulled her dark brows into a straight line. At their first meeting she had been intrigued by Emma, a tall, dark woman with a sensuous voice and eyes of a pale glittering blue. Peter had made the invitation and Cathy had gone eagerly to meet the woman who had fallen in love with her best friend. But within a few minutes she knew that she and Emma had nothing in common. Even worse, she sensed that Peter's future wife saw her as an enemy.

It had been a saddening occasion. Peter had tried so hard to act normally, but Cathy felt his defensiveness through every pore in her skin. Emma was by turns aggressive and silent, only coming to life when her brother's name came into the conversation. An event she made sure occurred frequently! Then she had been feverishly enthusiastic, hurling her observations like arrows; he was a man in a million, a superb athlete who had ridden and ski-ed before he could walk, so talented that noted academics spoke respectfully to him, of such personal attraction that he was always followed by a string of the most beautiful and desirable women in the world, all begging to share his bed.

Cathy watched the reckless smile with which Peter drained his glass and succumbed to temptation. Widening her eyes to their fullest extent she asked breathlessly, 'Gosh, he sounds *wonderful!* Almost like a fairytale! What does he do?'

Emma ignored Peter's half-choking laugh to stare blankly at Cathy's impossibly innocent face. Cathy smiled. 'Besides writing thrillers, I mean.' Her voice invested the words with delicate scorn.

Her hostess's expression became a nice compound of astonishment and fury. 'He's probably the best playwright of this century. Critics compare him to Shakespeare.' Emma paused impressively. 'The serial he wrote for television has been acclaimed as one of the most brilliant pieces of dramatic writing ever produced. It won every award of that year. And anyone who knows anything at all about literature knows that his plays are still going to be classics in two thousand years' time. His books are fun, a little bit of light relief for him, but even so they're very highly regarded.'

'How does he get the time?' Cathy's voice was guileless and smooth as cream. 'I mean, in between winning rodeos and chatting up moguls and picking his way through love-crazed women?'

Emma sent her a look in which bafflement warred with indignation. 'He does not ride in rodeos!' She gave a small, secretive smile but went on in a superior tone, 'He only needs about four hours' sleep a night. He's never slept much, not even when he was a child. My mother said that he never cried like other children, he just used to lie in his crib thinking. He was sent to a special boarding-schoold when he was four so that he could be exposed to the very latest and best teaching.'

'Oh, poor little boy,' Cathy cried with involuntary empathy, remembering only too well how she had hated boarding-school at first. But she had been ten! Her heart bled for the little boy taken from all the security he had ever known.

But Emma said impatiently, 'It didn't worry Jake! He's not like the rest of us, he doesn't need people, he's always been completely self-sufficient.' Her blue eyes raked Cathy's face in disparagement. 'That's why women go crazy about him, you know. He doesn't need them, he just enjoys them in a purely physical way. Really, he feels nothing but contempt for them when they fling themselves at him. If he ever marries it will be to a woman who can keep up with him, a woman as brilliant as he is.'

Cathy said, 'From what you've said, I doubt if there's one around!'

His adoring sister shrugged, saying calmly, 'Well, he'll want children. He likes them and he's good with them. As one of his professors said, he owes it to humanity to perpetuate his genes. He'll probably marry a woman who would make a good mother.'

Cathy, who believed that the only reason to have children was an overwhelming desire for them, decided shrewdly that Emma didn't want to see her brother married. Because the temptation was irresistible, she murmured, 'And they'll have little computers.'

It had not gone down at all well, especially when Peter's laughter joined hers. But it had been a cheap shot and Cathy was sorry now that she had allowed her irritation to get the better of her. After having met Jake Ferrers she understood a little better why his sister was so proud of him. Poor Emma had managed to make him sound quite insufferable, a genius with a lecher's calculating attitude towards women, admired more for the freakish quality of his mind than his character. But a man who had touched the hearts of millions of people could not be as cold and mechanical as that.

And he loved his sister; it was a measure of his love that he had come to her when she needed him. Endearing, but not sensible because of course the sensible thing to do would be to leave them to work out their own problems. Which, she supposed, was easy enough for an outsider to say. She recalled the suppressed pain in his voice when he had told her about Emma's childhood, and sighed.

Poor Peter, Cathy thought pensively, stretching out her legs to turn over on to her stomach. And poor Emma.

Above her a skylark shook a cascade of notes into the sparkling air.

She woke slowly, reluctantly, muttering a few words which in the jungles of Thailand mean, 'Not yet!'

A hand stopped shaking her shoulder; a masculine voice demanded in an arrested tone, '*What* did you say?'

The sound of that clipped accent brought her more quickly awake than anything else could have. She huddled away from the intrusive hand, forcing heavy lids upwards to meet Jake's sharp, inquisitorial stare.

Instinctively she took refuge in her sleepiness. 'What?' she muttered, covering a yawn with her hand while her brain got at last into gear.

'You said something in a language which was definitely not English. Something like Malay, I think. Perhaps one of the dialects of China.'

Slowly she shook her head. 'You must have misheard. I wasn't—I was asleep.'

She met his searching regard with a defiance which had a little boldness in it. It was important that he know nothing about the time she had spent in Asia. The impulse which had led her there, and the decision to stay, revealed too much about her; information which was classified. Cathy had been brought up to be distrustful. Over the years the lesson had been drummed into her until now she assumed it was an integral part of her character. How often she had heard her grandfather say that it was dangerous to let people understand how your mind worked, it made it easier for them to get the better of you!

And for some reason it seemed essential that she be very much on the alert where Jake was concerned.

He seemed to be able to sense her instinctive withdrawal for he frowned, his expression keen, but after a quick hard look he said, 'I thought you might like to learn how to milk the cow.'

His eyes were sliding boldly over her body, openly appreciating the contours of the soft curves beneath her clothes. Cathy said stiffly, 'Very well. When?'

'Now. It's five o'clock.'

She sat bolt upright, staring around her in consternation. Sure enough, the afternoon had that mellow, slightly sated ambience, a hushed peace as the day waited for the coolness of evening to bring refreshment.

'I don't normally sleep during the day,' she exclaimed, scrambling out of the lounger with as much grace as she could manage. 'Have you had any lunch?'

His gaze mocked her but he answered courteously enough, 'Yes, thank you, I found some cold meat to go with the salad you made.' A deeper shading of mockery in both eyes and voice. 'It was very good. Who taught you to cook?'

She returned his stare with an insolent one of her own before opening her eyes very wide. Innocently she purred, 'Why, it just comes naturally to me. I was born domesticated, you see.'

He gave a snort that turned into unwilling laughter but as she flashed him a cheeky grin before turning to go inside his hand flashed out to stop her. 'Let's call a truce, shall we, Cathy. I'm sorry if I've seemed overbearing and a trifle arbitrary——'

'A *trifle?*'

He grinned. 'That's all I'll admit to. I have a feeling that I'm going to need a fair amount of arrogance to get you to behave in a sensible way. However, I'm prepared to try to be conciliatory if you are.' He held out a hand.

Unconsciously Cathy bit her lip. After a stretched moment she put her own in his strong clasp, wondering a little desperately why she felt as though she had just signed away her birthright. Rather breathlessly she said, 'All right.' Adding as an afterthought, 'I wish you'd at least try to see that I'm not responsible for Emma's warped view of things.'

He frowned but waited a moment before admitting, 'I never said that you were. I know that she isn't the most rational of women. However, I think you should consider the fact that although she found marriage more difficult to adjust to than she expected, things didn't really start to go badly wrong until you came back. As long as you are around for Peter to cling to, you're making the situation worse.'

She could see that, yet he didn't seem able to understand that exactly the same thing could be said of him! Emma turned to him instead of trying to work things out with Peter. She stood looking up at him, her thoughts for once revealed in her face.

'Yes,' he said. 'I know, but I'm working on it. Trust me.'

Breathlessly she nodded.

His smile widened; he stood looking down at the small hand clasped in his dark fingers so she was never sure if it had been a gleam of satisfaction that his thick lashes hid so quickly.

She tugged free as he said, 'Right, friend. Now, we'd better get going. Mrs Stallworthy left a great long list of things that must be done before dusk.'

It was rather fun to call the hens in from around the garden and throw them grain; Cathy enjoyed their contented clucking noises and coy flutterings. When they had been shut safely inside their little house she went over to the small shed into which Jake and the golden Jersey cow had disappeared. Inside Jake sat, his lean hands moving competently beneath the patient cow, the milk hissing into a large bucket.

'What on earth do we do with all that milk?' Cathy asked in awe.

'Quite a bit goes to the pig, but Mrs Stallworthy makes cheese and butter and yoghurt from the rest.'

Cathy perched up on the bail, barely concealing her alarm. 'Do we have to do that?' she asked faintly.

His chuckle was pure masculine amusement, teasing yet warmly companionable. 'No, I conclude that we allow the pig to drink all that we don't want.'

Cathy turned to where the pig was rooting comfortably in his pen. 'The extra won't hurt him?'

'Most animals seem to know when to stop. It's only humans who are greedy.'

Cathy's vivid little face dimmed somewhat. Yes, she knew something about human greed. She turned back so that she could see the sea again and said, 'The Stallworthys live a self-sufficient sort of life, don't they? They must be busy all day. That is the most impressive vegetable garden I've ever seen, and their fruit trees are laden.'

'I imagine that living here would require a certain self-sufficiency,' he agreed.

'They love it. My grandfather used to say that they allowed us to come to their paradise out of the kindness of their hearts. For years I thought they really did own the island. Poor Mr Stallworthy. I do hope he's recovering. They'd hate it if they had to live in Auckland. He used to say that when you live in paradise where do you go for a holiday?'

He said nothing and she brooded on the caretaker and his pleasant practical wife for a few minutes before starting a little when his voice broke the silence.

'Here, you'd better try this. You never know when you may need to milk a cow!'

It was infinitely more difficult than she had imagined, but she set her mouth and followed his every instruction with intense care, because that way she could almost block out his closeness, and the way it affected her when he put his hand over hers to show her how it had to be done. Something strange was happening to her and she didn't want it, so she brought all her considerable powers of concentration to the task, and within a short time was rewarded by a white stream of milk going into the bucket.

'Look!' she crowed. 'Oh, look, I can do it!'

He laughed, his eyes never leaving her delighted face, then stood back so that she had the bucket to herself. For several minutes her small hands worked carefully until the unfamiliar motion began to cramp muscles never before used. Cathy turned her head and caught the smile which pulled at the corners of his hard beautiful mouth. Damn him! He was just waiting for her to admit that she could go no longer.

She set her mouth in a manner she had made her own, and went on carefully. Her knees began to ache, then the muscles in her forearms. A pain spread across her shoulders. She wriggled cautiously, wondering why she just didn't give in.

He knew, of course. But she gritted her teeth and kept at it until the flow of milk began to dwindle and he said calmly, 'I'll strip her out.'

Hard as she tried not to, she staggered as she rose from the stool. Instantly his hands gripped her shoulders, supporting, surprisingly gentle. He smelt of male, warm and tantalising and exotic, and there was a lurking, almost sympathetic understanding of her feelings in his eyes.

'A walk might help,' he suggested blandly.

So she went a few paces away where he couldn't see and opened and shut her sore hands, wincing at the pain in her maltreated muscles. In a voice she hoped was every bit as bland as his she asked, 'Where did you learn to milk a cow? It's not the sort of accomplishment one would expect from a literary genius.'

'I am not a genius,' he remarked matter-of-factly. 'You've been listening to Emma. I'd have thought that anyone with a normal amount of intelligence would discount the bias of a devoted sister. The school I went to believed that their students needed a firm foothold on reality as well as accelerated studies, so there was a farm attached to it. We all had duties, and we all learned to do them all. The man who looked after the farm was old, with his roots firmly in the past, so a lot of the things we were taught were not exactly practical in today's world of high-tech farming. Satisfying, though. I can also build a haystack and make a corn dolly.'

'Such a *useful* skill,' she observed, smiling.

Strong white teeth flashed as he laughed and stood up, opening the door of the bail with a long pole. 'Think of the rarity value. How many men do you know who can make a corn dolly?' he countered as he slapped the cow on the rump.

Cathy chuckled. 'Now that you mention it,' she said demurely, 'I can see that it's an accomplishment you could dine out on for years.'

'I have, believe me.' He picked up the bucket and set off towards the eager pig. Cathy followed, her eyes fixed on the swell of muscle across his shoulder and down his arm. His

movements, his carriage, were lithe and graceful and easy.
That strange, sharp sensation in the base of her stomach
gathered force, lancing up through her body to tighten her
breasts.

Desire. The warning signal. It was a common enough
sensation, and it could be extinguished. She narrowed her eyes
and tried to imagine the man in front of her in red and white
dotted briefs. To her surprise this usually infallible exercise
failed completely. No gurgle of laughter came to her throat.

Instead her mouth dried and she had to drag her mind away
forcibly from the image of him standing naked before her,
proud in all his predatory beauty, intent upon kindling her
latent passion.

Hastily swallowing she watched while he tipped the milk
into the trough in the sty, smiling as the pig squealed and
rushed across. It was a large white one with pink skin showing
through, and it had a cheerful brash smile. Cathy liked it
immensely, especially when it allowed her to scratch it behind
the ears.

'I thought pigs were dirty,' she said, looking around the
clean sty.

'Only when they're allowed to be. This one spends its life
out in the paddock and only comes in on winter nights. As you
can see, it keeps itself very clean.'

She nodded. It was that magic hour when the sun was going
down. Dusk was making its presence felt, gentle and cool as a
benediction. An early morepork called; Cathy looked up the
hill to the dark mass of the bush which was the small owl's
home, her heart swelling with joy. This was the place which
had filled her dreams for the last two years; this, she knew with
deep satisfaction, was home.

There was a ritual that belonged to the first night on the
island. But it, she thought as she walked back through the
quiet evening, would have to wait for darkness. And solitude.

CHAPTER FOUR

BY THE time Cathy decided it was safe to leave the house the little owl had given up calling in order to do some serious hunting. Shortly after they had eaten dinner Jake decided to go for a last look around the farm; she said hastily that as she was tired she would retire for the night.

He gave her a quick, assessing glance. 'In that case I'll turn in too,' he said.

The last thing she wanted was for him to see her go along the beach. The glow-worms had been her secret, her own special delight, ever since she had discovered them when she was only ten. Not even Peter knew of their existence. And she did not want Jake with her when she renewed her acquaintance with them.

So before she made any move she waited until the light in the cottage had been on for over an hour. Presumably by then he had settled down to whatever esoteric pursuits he occupied his evenings with. Feeling ridiculously like a burglar, she pulled a dark sweatshirt over her slacks and donned canvas shoes before slipping down the hill to the beach, treading with all the care of a hunting cat.

For the young Cathy the subterfuge, the secret trek through the darkness, had been an essential part of the glamour. Glow-worms were rarely visible during the day, so if she wanted to see them in all their splendour she had to sneak out when the adults had gone to bed. She had never been afraid of the dark, but even if she had been terrified she would have endured it to experience the magic.

Perhaps, she thought as she tiptoed along the beach past the cottage, she should thank Jake for providing her with a chance to recapture this forbidden, adrenalin-charged slice of her childhood!

Almost holding her breath she walked on, heading towards the part of the island which was still covered in bush. Glowworms, she had discovered in her reading, needed forest cover. They were often found in caves or banks, but only where there was thick vegetation above to keep the ground pleasantly moist through even the driest summer.

As she plodded through the yielding sand she remembered her excitement when she had discovered them, the breathless realisation that here, not more than half a mile from the bach, she had her own secret patch of the heavens to be enjoyed whenever she chose to visit them.

Just before she turned away from the beach she stopped and looked out to sea, the normal brilliance of her eyes soft with dreams as they swept the shores of the other islands, tiny sprinkles of light from distant windows fading into dark silhouettes which merged imperceptibly into distance and the night sky. The little stream at her feet gurgled softly before losing itself in the sand of the beach. Cathy smiled and turned away to scramble up the banks beneath the trees, waiting until she was well beneath the overhanging trees before she switched on the torch.

It was difficult progress up the gully; she had to step from rock to rock, setting her feet down cautiously. As she climbed, the noise of the creek increased about her until at last she came to a rift in the hill, deep and narrow and shadowy on even the sunniest day, where the water fell in leaps and bounds over what was almost a waterfall. Cathy found one particular boulder and sat down, switching off the torch and waiting for the peace and solitude to soak into her soul.

It was always a game to keep her eyes away from the bank until they were once more accustomed to the dark. As a child she had tired holding out for the count of a hundred, but never succeeded. She didn't manage it this time either. Smiling at herself, she lifted her eyes, and there they were, points of light in the dark bulk of the hillside, rows and rows of them, at first singly and then in clusters, in clouds, in constellations, each a small, steady glow in the darkness of the rocky wall. There were so many that they made their own light, a dim lessening of darkness in which she could just make out the pale splotch of her hand against the dark material of her slacks.

She sighed. Then shrieked, for Jake asked from close behind her, 'What are they?'

Her heart seemed to fly from her breast. She was so shaken that after that first short scream she couldn't speak, her tongue seemed to have cleaved to the roof of her mouth. Her hand flailed out and she slipped and landed on her knees with a splash in the water.

Instantly she was caught and pulled back up again. He said something under his breath then enfolded her shaking body in his arms, holding her against his broad warmth until the shuddering stopped and she could once more speak.

Then he said quietly, 'I'm sorry. I thought you knew I was there. I made no attempt to keep quiet.'

'No, I didn't hear you.' She pulled away, cold with an unknown emotion which frightened her. 'They're glow-worms,' she said, hiding her unease with a brisk voice. 'Native to New Zealand and Australia.'

'I see.' He was not looking at the lights; she could feel his eyes on her, watchful through the darkness. 'This is a favourite place of yours.'

'Yes.' She wasn't going to tell him that until then possibly no one else had ever seen this colony.

'How did you find it?'

Some of the rigidity left her but she hesitated before telling him, 'I was exploring on a particularly gloomy day, and I saw a few. I crept back that night and couldn't believe my eyes.'

'And you've come back ever since.'

'Wouldn't you?'

It came out as belligerence. However, his reply was level, almost without expression. 'Oh, yes. Do you know anything about the insect that produces the light?'

'It's a native gnat. The light comes from the back of the caterpillar. They dangle sticky threads down as a snare to lure tiny insects, then eat them. Would you like to have a look? If you touch one it will die, but unlike the ones in the Waitomo Caves they don't mind if you shine the torch at them, or make a noise.'

With unfeigned interest he went over to the rocky face, directing the beam on to a cluster of the small insects. Cathy sat on her boulder and watched the absorbed slash of his profile against the light; she should be resenting him for following her to this special place, yet her emotions were in a state of flux. It seemed like an obscure treachery to enjoy his company, but she did.

When he came back she moved automatically over so that there was room for him on the boulder. Accepting the tacit invitation, he switched off the light before settling his long form down beside her. Silently they sat looking at the myriad lights, listening to the surging splash and chuckle of the creek, conscious of the life all around them in the darkness. It was very peaceful, yet Cathy was prickly with awareness of the man beside her, and whereas before the glow-worms had always been enough she now found her attention wandering.

Eventually she began to shiver; since her stint in the tropics she felt the cold much more severely. Immediately Jake got to his feet.

'Time to go home,' he said, for all the world as if he were her father.

It should have antagonised Cathy, but it made her feel warm and cherished. A derisory little smile touched her mouth as she wondered whether she was in any danger because this hard man had a protective streak in him somewhere.

'Careful,' he said laconically half-way down as she stumbled.

'Too many city pavements, Cathy?'

On his tongue her name was a lazy caressing drawl that wound its way pleasantly through her nerves, setting them even more atingle. Cathy tried a tentative laugh. 'Perhaps,' she said demurely, thinking of the paths in the camp, dry and dusty half the year, ankle-deep in mud for the rest.

They walked the rest of the way to the beach in silence, and once out from beneath the trees stopped in unspoken agreement to savour the salt openness of the air. The dividing line between bush and farm came at the end of the bay; above them loomed the ramparts of a great fortified *pa* built hundreds of years ago when the Maori people held the land by right of discovery. Long deserted when the first European set eyes on the island, its inhabitants had been carried off by the near-constant warfare of those times. Now sheep pattered over the trenches and ramparts, and few people claimed descent from the original owners of the land.

'Who owns the sheep?'

Cathy said, 'They come from a farm over on Waiheke. The island is used as a run-off. They are barged back and forth.' And in case he asked who owned the farm, because she didn't want to admit that it was hers, she said softly, 'This place is haunted by a Maori woman who was killed here when she stole down to meet her lover.'

'Really?' His voice was dry.

She chuckled. Clearly a man who didn't believe in ghosts. 'So my grandfather was told. She was going to run away but her lover had brought a war party with him so he could do a little bloodletting on the side.'

'An opportunist,' he observed, even more drily.

She nodded. 'Apparently. However, her father was a suspicious man and he had her watched. When she crept away that night he and his warriors were hot on her trail. Legend has it that when she realised that her lover had betrayed her she rushed back towards the *pa* to warn her father and before he could save her one of the lover's men killed her to stop her from giving them away. Then her father and his men killed them all.'

Her voice was deliberately flippant because the sad tale always touched some hidden part of her soul.

'And she haunts this place?'

'Well, not here. Further up the gully where she was killed. She's supposed to weep because her lover betrayed her. She doesn't haunt women, but there have been stories about men who sense her presence.'

'And do you believe it?'

Her slight shoulders moved. 'I don't know. Isn't there a theory that strong emotions might be able to imprint themselves on their surroundings? Like grooves in a record? Emotions must have been running pretty high that night.'

'That,' he said in his driest tone, 'is probably an understatement.'

It was a very silent Cathy who walked beside him in the sea-scented darkness. She had grown up in a family where domination was both an art and a science. Sir Peter had used power as a bludgeon, only slightly tempering it where he loved. Cathy's mother had been infinitely more subtle, hiding that same lust to rule with an outwardly affectionate gentleness.

Cathy had spent her childhood trying to live up to goals set by a mother for whom no standards were high enough. Her adolescence had been a battle for autonomy; it was no wonder she had grown up fiercely suspicious and aggressive and arrogant. Living under emotional siege had made her protective of even innocent pleasures, for her mother had used those to try to control her. Trust came slowly to her; only Peter had ever been admitted to the inner recesses of her heart.

So she was bewildered by this *rightness* she felt as she walked by Jake's side through the scented darkness. Almost, she thought wonderingly, as though I trust him!

Which was ridiculous; the idea made her tremble with a

secret fear, yet that strange sense of oneness remained even when she glanced surreptitiously sideways and was struck again by the unnerving contrast of her own fragility against his strong frame. She was so glad to see the bach appear above them that she didn't try to hide the curtness of what was clearly a dismissal, saying, 'I'll see you tomorrow morning.'

But he prevented her escape. Strong fingers imprisoned her small wrist and in a voice laced with cool amusement he drawled, 'Are you going to help me milk the cow at half past six?'

Horrified, she retorted, 'Never, I'm no masochist! I'll practise in the afternoons.'

He laughed and pulled her into him, tipping her head with a casual hand in the curls at the back of her head. The other came up and traced an outline of the mouth he had crushed beneath his not so long before. Cathy, who had been fighting to banish the memory, trembled.

'I'm sorry.' The words were a smoky whisper on the sensitive skin of her lips. 'I have a lousy temper, and that aristocratic touch-me-not air you assume rouses every one of my baser Colonial instincts.'

'I thought you were English,' she said, so bemused by his closeness that she barely understood what she was saying.

He gave a soft chuckle. 'No. I was born on the West Coast. My father was a doctor there. After my primary school education they took me to England because they thought the opportunities were greater. Am I forgiven for my assault this afternoon?'

'What? Oh, yes.' She summoned up all her resolution and made a real effort to pull away but it was too late.

This time the kiss was almost gentle. At least, it started that way. Jake's mouth touched hers with a seducing sweetness which vanished almost immediately, smothered by an outburst of sheer, fiery sensation. Cathy went under without a protest, lost in the cascades of sensation which drowned her in a voluptuous pleasure.

A long time later he said in a shaken voice, 'What the hell do you do to me?'

And kissed her again, in a starving, desperate fashion which set alarm bells ringing in the dizzy, turbulent reaches of Cathy's brain. She gave herself up to the magic he was wreaking on her because it was impossible to resist, but when he lifted his head to search out the erotic little spot beneath her ear she whispered, 'Jake, we're going too fast. I—we have to stop.'

His face was buried in her throat. She could hear a muted thunder which was the blending of two heartbeats, and when she opened her eyes the lights along the horizon swooped and dipped. The swift pang of desire had flowered into something rare and bewildering, something which left her tormented and aching with a shattering pleasure. All the delights of paradise beckoned her in the form of the man who held her against the lean strong angles of his body, shocking her into an awareness of his masculinity as no other man had ever done before.

At last he said slowly, 'Yes, you're right.' He let her pull out of that fierce grip but his hand stopped her when she would have fled inside.

'This is not the end,' he said slowly, almost as if that quick brilliant mind had been as overcome by the fumes of passion as had hers. 'I don't have to tell you that I want you.'

She could say nothing, and after a pause he went on, with a little more clarity to the words, 'And it's quite obvious that you want me. I agree that we're going too fast, but I'm not going to back away from this, Cathy.'

She didn't know what to reply. When she looked up her eyes were caught by the compelling heat of his. In the starlight he looked like a god, one of the old heroes with virile strength and power emblazoned in his face. Her eyes wonderingly traced the strong line of jaw, the mouth which had given such pleasure, with its disciplined upper lip opposed so provocatively to the curved, beckoning lower one.

Caution warred with a new excitement in her heart. Without volition her hand stole out and touched his.

'Very well,' she said almost shyly.

On her arm his fingers bit, then relaxed. 'Willing to take a chance?'

And she said rashly, 'On you, yes.'

A primitive triumph lit his expression. 'I'll see you in the morning.'

It took her a long time to get off to sleep but she woke the next morning to a day which made all her forebodings of the day before seem paltry, the night terrors of a coward. Lured by the gold of the morning, she ran out through the unlocked doors to stand in joyful delight on the terrace, her bare toes curling on to the wet bricks.

Sunlight shimmered across an opalescent sea, blue and silver and green mingling into a colour like nothing she had seen before. Bees were shrill with early-morning zest in the jasmine flowers, sending little wafts of the sensuous perfume through the warming air. High in the bare branches of the flame tree a tui pealed his courtship song, the brilliant iridescent blues and greens of his plumage a sharp contrast to the scarlet porcupine claws of the flowers he plundered. Thrushes sang with the voices of angels, a shrill sweet counterpoint to the petulant call of a gull out over the reef. The dissipating dew smelt fresh and new, like the beginning of the world.

Or a new life? Cathy wondered.

And out from the bay, about a mile away, a splendid three-masted ship dipped gracefully into the swell as she headed out towards the Barrier Islands, her sails as full as the petals of a rose. She was the new training ship, just launched to provide experience in sailing for the youth of the country. Smiling, Cathy went indoors to change from her long cotton nightgown into jeans and a sweatshirt before going out to help Jake.

In retrospect, she saw that that morning was the beginning

of her enchantment. True to their unspoken agreement, Jake made no effort to intensify their relationship but he didn't try to weaken it either. When they explored the island he held her hand, and each night before he retired to the cottage he kissed her until she was breathless and clinging, leaving her with a head full of dreams and an aching frustration which increased with each touch, each kiss.

He was immensely interesting; Cathy sometimes thought that she could listen to him for days, weeks, years, and never become tired of the deep, deliberate voice, the razor-sharp brain and the quick humour which struck sparks from her so that she astonished herself. For the first time in her life she had met someone who valued her intelligence, and because she wanted him to respect her she responded eagerly, as she had never talked to anyone before. She felt her mind expanding as she tried to keep up with his; it was exhilarating and inspiring, yet some wary residue from her childhood kept dammed the impulse to open herself entirely to him.

And she sensed that he too was not giving away all the secrets of his personality. In a way this rather pleased her even as it frustrated her. She had been conditioned to distrust the easy, artless response; she suspected that Jake thought the same. This slow discovery, flavoured with discussion, spiced with laughter, dangerously poised on the brink of falling into the seething abyss of passion which both recognised and neither was prepared to surrender to, this, she thought as golden day succeeded golden day, must be what falling in love was all about.

Passion was greedy, a sudden flashfire which burnt out as quickly as it came; her experience with Trent had proved that. What she and Jake were doing was laying foundations and building walls, and even though sometimes she felt her body ache with suppressed desire, she was happy to have it so.

It was a time for joy, one of those rare seasons when the rain came at night and the days were warm and soft with only gentle winds. And if occasionally Jake relapsed into an abrupt moodiness, well, Cathy understood that too, for she also had moments when she couldn't convince herself that this idyll was true. Waking in bed at night she would find her suspicious mind turning over incidents, picking out words and phrases for analysis, fretting and worrying in case it all proved to be a cruel joke.

But in the kind light of each day she realised how conditioned she had become for rejection, how wary, and she told herself that she was a fool, because whatever Jake had in mind for her was not betrayal. And her smile irradiated her face; she knew that when he made his move she would welcome him as her lover, for he was all that she wanted in a man. He might not be thinking of marriage; if he was, Cathy wasn't too sure that she was ready for that. But she was not going to spoil this enchanted time by worrying about the future. Each day was too golden with happiness for fear to spoil it.

Mr Stallworthy wrote to thank her for her flowers and her calls, telling her that he was recovering fast and would get better even quicker if they would only let him go back to the island. Alarmed, Cathy rang his wife and invented a sickness plan for all employees of the Durrant holdings, giving them another fortnight to be spent on the mainland so that when he came out of hospital he would be within reach of a doctor. From the eagerness with which Mrs Stallworthy greeted the idea Cathy realised that she too had been worrying that he might go back to work too quickly.

Peter contacted her several times, ostensibly to tell her that her plants were surviving his efforts with the watering-can. He sounded cheerful enough, but there was a dragging undertone to even his most flippant comments which made Cathy's heart ache. He said Emma was behaving reasonably well, and so was he. Jake, he mentioned once in passing, had gone off somewhere by himself. He was in the habit of doing that. No doubt to recharge his batteries.

Cathy smiled, a siren's smile as old as time, and told herself that if Jake didn't want his possessive sister to know where he was, who was she to tell?

He came in as the smile was fading, but of course he noticed. 'What,' he asked, amusement almost completely hiding a certain grimness, 'have you been up to?'

She knew the grimness would increase if she told him who she had been talking to, so she merely shook her head, mischief gleaming in a very distracting way in her face. No lies, she thought and told him what she had organised for the Stallworthys.

'Clever girl,' he drawled. 'So how much more time have we alone?'

She told him, then hesitated, a frown pulling her brows straight. 'I don't think I did it for that reason,' she objected after a moment's concentrated thought. 'Mrs Stallworthy was worried about bringing him straight back to the island, I could tell she wanted to stay a little longer at her sister's, just in case.' Another thought struck her. She sent him a wide, guileless glance. 'Of course you don't have to stay here. I can milk the cow now and feed the pig and hens, so if you want to go back to the mainland, do.'

His eyes narrowed, intensifying the stare he inflicted on her until she almost squirmed with tension. It took all her will-power to keep her expression open and innocent.

At last he observed on a hard note, 'That must be a great asset.'

'What?'

'The ability to look like a child whose innocence has never been questioned.'

She grinned. 'It has come in handy, I must admit. Most people were fooled by it. Even my grandfather, on occasion. Not Peter, however.' Hurried into finishing by the sudden harshness of his expression, she added, 'Or Trent.'

'Or me,' he said, almost as it it were a threat.

She smiled sunnily. 'Perceptive, aren't you.'

He laughed, and kissed her with finesse and a certain amount of ruthlessness so that her mouth softened into submission beneath the demand of his. 'Don't forget it,' he said, the words coming from deep in his throat.

Another warning? She thrust his words to the back of her mind and allowed herself to drift along, basking in the radiant promise of her newly roused emotions.

The harsh call of the telephone broke into her sleep the next morning and after the usual muttering and groaning she woke enough to realise that either the unnatural caller had hung up or Jake had answered it over at the house. Sighing heavily she groped about, finally located the receiver and lifted it to her reluctant ear.

It took a moment or two for her to recognise Emma's voice, hurrying through the words as though she didn't want to be caught speaking.

Before she had time to register anything that was said Cathy hung up, and sank back on to the pillows, her expression puzzled.

So Emma did know where Jake was. Well, she thought, persuading herself, so what? If she wasn't careful she could become as paranoid as her grandfather, who had seen treachery and betrayal everywhere, built his life on that perception, and died unloved and feared. Biting her lip, she pushed the ugly doubts to the back of her mind.

Her reward came later that morning when Jake said, 'Was that you on the phone when I was talking to Emma?'

Warmth flooded a heart she had refused to admit was cold. 'Yes, I'm sorry, I thought the call was for me.'

'She rang to tell me I've been invited to a bash given by the local branch of a conglomerate I did some work for.'

'Oh.' She was extremely curious, but of course good manners forbade any question.

He gave her a quizzical smile. 'Would you like to go?'

'I——' A part of her wanted to stay here, where nothing and nobody could interrupt their idyll, but she abandoned caution for the truth. 'Very much. What sort of affair is it going to be?'

'Formal. I judged a short story contest they sponsored and they want to present the results with as much publicity as possible. Which means all the local and political notables and white tie.'

'And when is it?'

'Three days after the Stallworthys get back. That should give them time to settle in.'

It did too. Although, even to his wife's concerned eyes, it was clear that Mr Stallworthy was one of those people who suffer few ill effects from an operation. He was eager to get back to work, and it was only Jake's presence that persuaded the older man to take it easy. And even then he had to see for his own eyes that Jake was capable.

'Better able to do everything than he is,' his wife grumbled the morning after their arrival as she watched both men walk across the paddock. 'So am I, if it comes to that.'

Cathy chuckled. 'So am I. Jake taught me how to milk the cow.'

Mrs Stallworthy looked significantly at her. 'You're looking very well. Come home for good, have you?'

'I don't know.' The words came slowly. Not even to herself would Cathy admit the inchoate fears and hopes which still swirled in the depths of her subconscious.

That night, after Jake left her, she wondered if she should be upset that in three whole weeks he had not once tried to persuade her into bed. She knew perfectly well that it was not through lack of ardour; the kiss they exchanged each night reassured her of that. Jake's response was undisguised; she accepted his involuntary reaction to her closeness with a complete understanding, because although less obvious, her own response was every bit as strong.

And Jake knew. He was experienced in the ways of a

woman's body, she could tell from the way he kissed and touched her, the slow, caressing seduction of his hands and mouth. Experienced and with a natural genius in this as well as writing, she thought, trying hard for her usual flippancy to cover the wildness which built inside her each time their eyes met. He must know that if he applied the heat she might begin by resisting, but eventually she would surrender.

And he was not held back by any knowledge that she was a virgin. He knew of her marriage; like everyone else he would think that it had been normal. After all, Trent was an experienced, virile man.

This could mean only one thing. Jake didn't want an affair. For him as well as her it was something new, something which he wanted to make strong and lasting.

It was this knowledge which gave her expression such a luminous glow. She was not alarmed because Mrs Stallworthy recognised it, but she hoped that her feelings were not quite so obvious to Jake. In spite of her efforts to banish it the old caution, the fear of rejection, was still lurking behind the door, barely concealed by her incandescent happiness.

Probably because she marvelled that out of all of the women in the world Jake should have chosen her. He was so magnificent, and she was really very ordinary. Oh, attractive enough, in a sultry, sulky way; she had her mother's superb skin and her voluptuous figure attracted men, but she wished that she was truly beautiful so that men looked at her the same way women looked at Jake, with a kind of awe beneath the speculation and the interest because he was all alpha male, so confident in his own masculinity that he didn't ever have to think about it.

And with a kind of bone-deep animal magnetism which transcended the outer attractive features, the striking face and magnificently built body, it was no wonder that she should be finding herself perilously close to surrender. Not even to herself did she whisper the word love; if anyone had asked her she would have said that perhaps only a few very lucky people ever attained real love, and she doubted whether it would ever come her way.

In the meantime she was content to drift with the warm tides of summer, showing Jake the island as if it were a present she could give him in all its blue and green and gold beauty, at once lazy and pastoral yet with a stark beauty emphasised by the brilliant clarity of the light. They swam together in the cove and walked the hills until the hot sun forced them to sit under a tree and look out across the water. Cathy pointed out the other islands and showed him the shipping lanes, told him the euphonious Maori names of the hills on the mainland, from sacred Moehu at the end of the Coromandel Peninsula to twin-humped Tamahuhu on the mainland, forty miles north of the white suburbs of Auckland.

He said idly, 'You know an extraordinary amount about the Gulf.'

She was sitting with her arms hugging her shins, her chin resting on her brown knees. It was very hot and they had climbed through bush to the bare knoll which was the highest peak on the island. 'I love it here,' she returned dreamily.

'That's obvious.' And surprising, his tone intimated.

She looked through her lashes. He was lying on his back with an arm over the upper part of his face, so that all she could see of it was the straight line of his mouth, disciplined, severe. A strange little chill feathered through her nerves. 'Haven't you any place that you call your own?'

'No. Oh, property, bought for convenience and investment, but no place that I enjoy as much as you do this.'

He spoke little of himself but she had gathered that he lived in a flat in London and owned a house in the Seychelles where he did a lot of his writing. Watching him with ardent eyes she wondered what it would be like to be so rootless.

'I think everyone should have a *turangawaewae*, a place to stand, a home place,' she said after a moment. 'It gives one stability, a sense of belonging.'

'Instead, most people scrimp and save for a roof over their head, forced to live in dreary suburbs and work at jobs they dislike, for a wage that never stretches as far as they want it to.'

There was a note in his voice which grated across her impulse to confide. Diffidently she suggested, 'But not you.'

'No, nor you. Both of us unfairly honoured by whatever gods presided at our christenings. Does it ever worry you that you have so much and others so little?'

She was too taken aback at the sudden savage note in his voice to answer sensibly. As she sat trying to formulate a reply she realised that he was watching her with flat opaque eyes.

After a strained moment he laughed without humour. 'No, why should it? Life for you is wonderful, why should you be concerned about those who are less fortunate than you are?'

Perhaps she should have trusted him enough to tell him then but some remnant of arrogance stopped the words even as they came tumbling from her indignant mouth and then it was too late, the moment of truth had gone.

Indifferently he said, 'Sorry, I'm afraid I tend to get on my hobbyhorse a bit.'

Cathy permitted herself a small cynical smile. 'Oh,' she said with airy sarcasm, 'I like to see signs of a social conscience in rich men, it gives them such depth and interest! Tell me, in what worth-while way did Emma occupy her time before she decided to take up making Peter miserable as her life's work?'

He had closed his eyes and she watched with real enjoyment as they flew open at her direct attack. She smiled. It was a syrupy smile, patently false, insolent and feline at the same time, guaranteed to infuriate any man. A cold anger splintered into shards in the depths of his gaze. For a long tense minute they locked horns, neither giving an inch.

Until, with a reluctance so obvious she could feel it, he drawled, 'I said I was sorry.'

'So you did,' she agreed, spuriously sweet. 'Perhaps you

should practise infusing your voice with meaning when you say these things. Say, ten times before breakfast every morning? A less sincere apology I've never heard.'

In a smooth movement which took her completely by surprise he sat up and reached out a long arm, ignoring her squeak of dismay as he hauled her on to his lap. She was beginning to object vociferously when he silenced her protests by the simple expedient of crushing them to silence on her lips.

This was not the embrace she had grown to expect from him. Gone was the restraint she counted on; in its place white-hot passion. His mouth forced hers open, tipping her head back into the angle of the arm that held her clamped in place, and his tongue thrust deep in startling and erotic mimicry of the ultimate conquest.

Cathy had always hated deep kisses, feeling suffocated and repelled when other men had tried to force them on to her, but she had learned to respond with ardour and a wild thrill of desire to Jake's mouth. This, however, was not passion, this was naked aggression, a predator's slaking of a hunger that was entirely one-sided. Struggling vainly against his anger and her weak impulse to surrender, she felt the first real stirrings of panic blend in with a wild, unwilling response.

But her frantic resistance went for nothing; he kissed her as though there were to be no tomorrow, his heated mouth avid and brutal against her skin, bruising her lips and then the long line of her throat while his hands tightened about her, holding her small body prisoner against the hard insistence of his.

The worst thing about it was that although her mind demanded that she resist her body thrilled with a primitive answer, his predatory maleness calling to something earthy and feminine in her. It mingled with the fear to drown her in a flashflood of sensation, until the fear was gone and she could only moan in his arms and give him a response so heightened beyond her normal experience she felt she had been translated into another dimension.

At last he seemed to realise that he was possessed of some kind of madness, for he groaned and lifted his head from the soft thunder of the pulse in her throat.

Cathy lay quiescent, her lashes casting shadows on the pale skin beneath her eyes. Heat seared her body; her tongue tentatively touched the stinging skin of her lips. Yet she was not angry, no longer afraid.

'I'm sorry,' he groaned and this time there was no mistaking the honesty of the words.

Yet he didn't release her, holding her almost convulsively against the throbbing length of his body until she said, 'It's all right, I was being as provocative as I could be.'

Then his arms loosened and he rolled away, self-disgust weighing down his words as he said slowly, 'You seem to bring out the worst in me.'

There was something thrilling in this knowledge; something worrying too. Instinct warned her to play it lightly. Infusing her tone with a casual cheerfulness she said, 'And you in me, I'm afraid.'

For a moment he lay rigid, the long line of his back expressing complete rejection, then he sat up and gave her an amused, totally cynical look. 'Does nothing perturb you?'

'Not a lot,' she returned smoothly, letting out a long-held breath with great care.

And it was over, but the incident cast its shadow over the rest of their stay. On the surface nothing had changed, but Cathy missed the closeness which had so warmed her heart. Once more she tried to convince herself that she was too sensitive, seeing shadows where none existed; by sheer force of will she almost managed to repress her illogical fears. Jake was just as charming, every bit as fascinating; each evening he kissed her with the same hungry passion.

It was, she told herself severely, a carry-over from the

ingrained suspicions of her childhood that sensed a hidden deliberation in the way he regarded her.

CHAPTER FIVE

THE ferry trip back to Auckland was swift and exciting; Cathy lifted a glowing face to the sun, uncaring that the wind was tearing her hair into shreds of vivid silk, trying not to see that the amusement in Jake's aquamarine eyes was tempered by a darker, more guarded emotion.

'When we came across in my grandfather's cruiser I used to wriggle out and sit on the bow,' she said reminiscently. 'I had to sneak up there and hide because my grandmother was convinced I'd fall over and drown. But I always tried, and they always found me and brought me back kicking and screaming.'

'Was a tantrum your usual method of dealing with any attempt at discipline?'

She turned an indignant gaze to meet the irony in his smile, admitting, 'Like all kids, I had the occasional one.'

'Until when?'

'Until someone I respected very much pointed out to me that tantrums were inexcusably childish.'

'And who,' he asked aloofly, 'was that? Trent Addison?'

'Right first time.' As always when Trent was mentioned her tone was incorrigibly flippant. It served to hide the guilt.

'It's strange that you and he and his wife are "all good friends" still.'

'Well, it's only civilised,' she said, hiding rather well the uneasiness that threaded through the words.

'I doubt that I should feel quite so civilised about the whole matter. Especially if I were in his wife's place. After all, comparing you clinically, she is attractive in a splendidly Junoesque style but you have a much earthier, more basic appeal. A man could like Melly Addison; I doubt if a man has ever put you and the concept of liking in the same sentence together.'

Her back stiffened. On the surface of it the words had been a compliment, but there had been a current of something she rather thought was distaste running through the words.

Aloofly she said, 'Melly knows I'm no threat to her marriage. You must have seen that Trent loves her with a—well, he loves her very much.'

'More than he did you?'

She looked up at the relentless angles of his profile, slashed hawklike and arrogant against the luminescence of silver sea and sky of azure, and wondered rather desperately how they had got on to this subject, and how she was going to get them off it. Again she felt that uneasy premonition, as though he was manoeuvring the conversation towards some unstated goal, and again she dismissed it.

She evaded the question lightly. 'I was very young when I married him.'

'And he, so I've heard, was very ambitious.'

The casual observation stung like a whip. This too she had done, made Trent a subject for snide comments. He had never shown that the gossip worried him in any way, but she hated knowing that her wilfulness was still affecting him. That, at least, she could deny.

Trying to speak calmly she said on a note of suppressed passion, 'Trent did *not* marry me so that he could gain control of my grandfather's businesses. That is a lie, and a particularly mean one, as anyone who knows Trent is well aware.'

'So why did he marry you?'

The laconic question made her bite on her lip a second before she said flatly, 'That's my business.'

He seemed to accept that, although a nervous glance from beneath her lashes revealed a faint curve to his lips which could have been the beginnings of a smile—not a pleasant one, she knew instinctively.

Fortunately at that moment the freighter which had just rounded one of the buoys behind them let out a long mournful wail on its siren which made her jump, and before she had recovered her poise one of the big tourist catamarans rounded North Head, blue and white striped sails set, and by the time she had exclaimed over it and answered his questions, the subject was well and truly left behind.

Yet a trace of uneasiness remained throughout the business of negotiating the run up-harbour and the settling of the ferry into its berth. Cathy found herself watching Jake, searching his features for clues to the thoughts behind that handsome face.

It was impossible. Jake allowed few emotions to make any impact on the handsome mask of his face. To all outward appearances he was a striking man with a woman he found very attractive; his eyes lingered on her face with appreciation and enough desire to make her flush, and he made it more than obvious that she was with him, directing a look as cold and dangerous as an ice-pick at one man whose eyes lingered too long on her breasts. Clearly shaken, the man had swallowed nervously and turned away.

The car was waiting in the car park, an opulent Jaguar. As she allowed herself to be settled into it Cathy caught the eye of a girl of about eighteen or so, a plain, lumpy girl dressed without discretion in jeans and a floppy T-shirt. Emotion flamed for a moment in the girl's stare, a naked, bitter envy which made Cathy drew her breath sharply. Then the girl turned away and Cathy sank back into her seat, strangely, deeply shaken by the tiny incident.

She knew what the girl had seen. Two beautiful people unfairly endowed with more than the world's treasures, enjoying each other's company, perhaps in love. Everything that publicity had convinced her was valuable and desirable. And because she saw no hope of getting any of it, she had been searingly resentful.

If only she knew, Cathy thought. Looking back, her life seemed to her to be one long saga of rejection and failure. The money Sir Peter had gained by fair means and foul meant little to her, no more than it had to him. Power was what he had hungered for; the money was only a by-product, a means to an end. Power he achieved, but he had died a lonely old man. Like him, Cathy felt that she had nothing to show for her life. If she died tomorrow Trent and Peter would probably be sorry; she couldn't honestly think of anyone else who would miss her, and there was no one for whom she came first. No one who loved her.

Wondering desolately what Jake felt for her, she sent a swift glance upwards. She had hoped that he too was coming under the sway of this tender emotion which had budded so secretly, so silently, in her heart. But after that bout of ferocious lovemaking on the hill he had been imperceptibly retreating to some remote mental fastness, and she was left to wonder if she had been harbouring dreams and indulging in dangerous fantasies.

Oh, God, she thought urgently, childishly, *make* him like me, at least. I know I haven't much to offer a man like Jake, but I'll give him everything I have.

After he dropped her off at her apartment with a crooked smile which didn't lighten the darkness at the back of his eyes, she watched him drive away with a kind of bleak foreboding chilling her blood.

Ridiculous, she told herself stoutly. She was being stupid, over-reacting, too sensitive. Her heart gave a strange little jerk, almost of pain.

Wasn't it supposed to be the high point of a woman's life, this first tentative step towards love? Shouldn't she be seeing rainbows and hearing birds trill at impossible times? She looked around, but the only rainbow was dyed into the hair of a girl who was walking down the opposite side of the road, and the nearest thing to birdsong was the cacophany of sound erupting from the ghetto blaster she carried.

Cathy gave a nervous little laugh and went inside. The apartment smelt stuffy; she looked around it with a nose unconsciously wrinkled, surprised to realise that she hated its confined space, no garden, no view from the windows but roads and houses . . . At least Peter's assiduous watering had kept the plants green and healthy. She would have to get the key back from him; it was her only spare.

Momentarily she grimaced, remembering Jake's comment about eighties chic. Her lawyer had rented the apartment for her because he thought it was safer for a single woman of obvious wealth, but she knew a sudden hunger for a house of her own, with a garden around it.

Soon, she promised herself as she searched through her wardrobe for a dress to wear to this formal dinner and dance.

After half an hour she decided that nothing was suitable. For some inexplicable reason she wanted something new. A symbol? Perhaps.

Five minutes later she was walking down the hill towards Parnell Village, a collection of boutiques and speciality shops housed in splendidly restored villas and houses of the last century. As usual it was crowded with tourists and shoppers; Cathy wandered for a little while, watching happily as groups of people merged and separated, laughed and told each other of bargains. Finally she went purposefully up a flight of stairs to a small cupboard of a shop which she had noticed in one of her previous forays to the Village.

Half an hour later she was walking back home with an expression which could only be described as faintly smug. Although most of the clothes in the tiny boutique had apparently been designed for giraffes, she had been lucky enough to find exactly what she wanted. The dress, if one could refer to it by such a mundane term, was stunning. With pleasure she pictured Jake's face when, clad in it, she opened the door to him.

Its effect was all she could have desired. For a moment too swift to be savoured, his reactions were obvious; she almost gasped at the shock of open desire which blazed forth as his eyes swept the length of the black lace, lingering on the deeply plunging neckline and the tight waist of the timelessly beautiful, shamelessly enticing dress.

Almost immediately he regained control but something of his first reaction still lingered in the depths of his eyes. Cathy didn't attempt to hide her small, satisfied smile, and he laughed.

'In some ways you haven't grown up much,' he said coolly. 'I shan't inflate your ego, however. All children have to learn that too many compliments are bad for the character.'

She grinned. 'You don't have to flatter me, although I must say I think you are mean. It took me an hour to get ready.'

'Really?' His voice was bland and she could almost have thought him unaffected except for the lingering embers which gleamed in the depths of his eyes. 'Then I won't spoil the effect by kissing you—or touching you.'

She contrived to look scandalised. 'Well, of course not! You don't think I went to all that trouble for you, do you? Everyone knows that women dress for other women!'

Her audacity was rewarded with a sidelong smile, at once conspiratorial and mocking. 'Really? I think I might enjoy disproving that. Later.'

The evening was an enchantment, a heady blend of laughter and flirtation and excitement; Cathy scintillated. Her fears were dissipated like the dew in the morning sun. Jake seemed to be as proud of her as she was of him, and all the time the sexual awareness hummed between them, sparkling in Cathy's eyes so that they were the glittering colour of the sea in high summer, giving a richer curve to the mouth which could look sulky or sultry and now became tender and full. Dimly, she recognised other people; she even spoke to them and she supposed what she said made sense, as none of them looked askance at her, but she felt that they were not really alive, they were wraiths hovering outside the magic world she and Jake made for themselves.

He was charming and amusing, teasing and exciting, and beneath that common coinage of the world they inhabited, he was all primitive male, his lean body poised and waiting for what she knew now was to be her inevitable surrender.

The thought should have terrified her, but she had crossed some Rubicon of the will and although she didn't know it, her every movement, every gesture spoke of surrender.

When at last the dinner and the speeches were over a band began to play. Jake smiled into her dazzled face and took her hand, leading her across to the polished parquet floor under the envious or sympathetic eyes of those around them.

Neither noticed. When they reached it Cathy relaxed against him with a little sigh of relief. It had become unbearable, that wild hunger clawing at her, and for a while the sensation of being held close against him eased it.

Her eyelids drifted down, heavy with unspoken, unhidden desires. Some last sensible part of her mind was relieved because the dimness of the room ensured that nobody would be able to see the expression on her face; she was past concealing the frightening, thrilling sensations which enslaved her.

Silently, gracefully, they moved together, he commanding, dominating her small form in a dance of passion and surrender. Once she looked up at him, noting with a strange detachment the inscrutable angles of his face, until her gaze was caught by the brilliance of his eyes, narrowed and glittering beneath the black lashes.

He said nothing, she made no sound, but in that long burning look a question was asked and answered. Mutely she walked beside him across the room. She smiled, said farewells, and, still smiling, went out into the night with him.

He took her home, and once inside the door turned her to

him as though he could wait no longer, his arms contracting around her willing body in an embrace as fierce as it was painful. Cathy gave a soundless gasp and lifted her face, her lashes fluttering down, excitement running like electricity through every nerve in her body. Yet he did not kiss her.

At last, in surprise and bewilderment, she opened her eyes, to gaze up into a face so harsh in the faint light that it looked like a primitive cast made for some fearsome religion. The febrile lights glinting in his eyes should have reassured her but she felt a cold pang of fear rip through the heated anticipation which encompassed her.

Almost silently she said his name, unaware that her emotions were written on her face.

'Tell me,' he commanded.

She said, 'What?'

'Tell me what you're feeling.'

She whispered, 'I want you.'

Something dangerous hooded his gaze. 'How?' he asked, his lips barely moving. 'In your bed, Cathy? In your body? Or just for a few kisses and a little heavy petting? You chose that dress deliberately to emphasise all your very desirable feminine attributes, so that any man who looked at you tonight would know what you have on offer. Tell me exactly what it is.'

She whitened, then colour came rushing back into her skin. 'You know,' she said painfully.

'I have to be sure I've read your signals correctly. I'm no tame boyfriend to be made happy with a few kisses and caresses. If I kiss you I'm going to take you, and when you wake up in the morning it will be as my woman.'

Her lip caught in her teeth, she stared at him, as implacable as iron, as hard to penetrate. Then, slowly, because she had never said it before, she whispered, 'I want you as my lover. And when I wake tomorrow morning it will be with a smile.'

Triumph flamed into life in his eyes. He bent his head and kissed her startled eyes shut, his mouth soft and oddly persua-

sive, as different from the hard line of a moment before as
anything could be.

Cathy's doubts and fears fell away. Whimpering deep in her
throat, she pushed against his hard strength, tormented by the
need which racked her. He responded, his body becoming taut
with the same excitement which exploded through her every
nerve-end. Her hands caught at the material of his shirt,
pulling at the studs until he laughed beneath his breath and
picked her up and took her through to the bedroom, where he
set her on her feet beside the bed.

Each movement a promise as explicit as that which gleamed
in his narrowed eyes, his hands found the fastenings of her
dress. She drew in a deep obstructed breath. Her body swayed
languorously, inviting him to finish what he had begun. Yet he
stopped, his expression enigmatic, and stepped away.

'Undress for me,' he said.

Cathy felt her skin heat beneath that molten stare, but she
wanted to show him how much she trusted him, and she
wanted more than anything to wipe that aura of control from
him, to see him trembling, as naked to the onslaught of passion
as she was.

Moving with deliberate provocation she slid the zip down,
arching her body in innocent grace, not fully aware of the
sensuous promise in the subtle, slow movements.

The man watching her felt his body clench in an agony of
need. His breath caught in his throat as slowly, her every
movement an assurance of untold delights, she stripped for
him.

First was the exquisite dress, dropped carelessly to the floor.
Cathy stepped out of her shoes, glad that she hadn't worn
stockings, and unclasped her bra. She should have been shy,
awkward, but an unashamed pride in her body, in the gift she
was about to give him, held her head high, gave colour to her
cheeks and a smile to her mouth. It was strangely, powerfully
erotic to stand almost naked in front of him: she felt wild and

free, as potently elemental as a force of nature.

The glow of the lamp gleamed golden across her breasts, picked out the indentation of her waist, turned the length of her thighs to amber. All woman, she smiled, innocently inciting, eager to taste the pleasures in store. Jake stood like a statue hewn in bronze, only the leaping lights in his eyes revealing his emotions.

'Dear heaven, Cathy,' he said in a harsh, impeded voice.

She stared at him, trying to read what was going on behind that dark formidable face. That he wanted her was obvious; their mutual hunger throbbed through the quiet room, almost tangible, so strong that she fancied she could feel it beating against her skin. Yet she grew wary, her expression shadowed, because she sensed that something was not right.

'Cathy,' he said. It was almost a plea, but then he cursed swiftly, 'Damn you!'

And he was tearing his shirt off to reveal the splendid masculine torso, the oiled ripple of muscle golden in the light of the lamp, powerful and imbued with a perilous male symmetry which drove all thoughts from Cathy's mind.

Her mouth dried; she put out a shaking hand and touched his chest, her fingers curling through the dusting of hair to the fiery skin beneath. Jake's mouth contorted; he swore and held her hand still, while he stood still, his head bowed, his eyes abstracted and remote and cold as agony.

Then he looked up, and instantly the frightening bleakness was gone, replaced by such passion that it drew his face into a bronzed mask, hard and primeval so that Cathy took a step backwards, almost appalled at what she had roused.

'No,' he said huskily, and pulled her into the hot cage of his arms, kissing her mouth, opening it with a force she had no defences against, before he explored the sweet depths with an urgency that came close to desperation.

Cathy gave him everything that he demanded, surrendering to the hard force of his masculine hunger as she met passion with passion, fire with fire, incandescent with a need which took her from the world she had always inhabited into another where colours were brighter, richer, sensations incredibly magnified.

After timeless moments he lifted her in his arms and put her on to the bed, his mouth crushing hers as he followed her down.

Her hands smoothed over the strain of muscle beneath the smooth heat of his skin; she pushed to meld with him, lost in his taste and his erotic, musky scent, her wild eyes glazed. She cried out when he bit down the length of her throat, moaned as he made himself master of the soft, sensitive mounds of her breasts, taunting her with swift fleeting kisses until she thought she might die.

Then, when she thrust against him with her hips, commanding his entry, he made a strange low sound in his throat and his mouth fastened on to the tight bud of her nipple, suckling with a hungry enjoyment which almost hurt her.

His name broke from her lips in a dying whisper. She shuddered with pleasure, a pleasure which only increased when he did the same to the other one.

Pain began drawing at the apex of her body, pain which was at once an anguish and exquisite beyond anything else she had ever felt. It tightened, began to screw its way, unsatisfied and clamouring, through cells and nerves and bloodstream.

Her hands clenched, digging painfully into the muscles of his shoulders; she was unaware of it, unaware of anything but that it was imperative for this pain to be assuaged, eased in the only way possible.

Then she heard him say, 'No.'

And to her complete bewilderment he tore her arms from around his neck and pushed free of the bed to stand beside it.

Stunned, still at the mercy of the need that raged through her body, she lay for a moment like a dead thing, listening

with incredulous ears to the sound of her own pulses and the
harshness of his breathing. Emptiness began to twist around
her heart, sending its icy influence down the hidden pathways
of her body.

At last she pushed herself up on an elbow to look across at
him, hoping against hope that she would see something which
proved her horrible suspicions were wrong.

He was standing still, looking towards the door, his only
movement the rise and fall of his chest as he fought for control.
The features of his face were drawn into a mask, forbidding
with a savagery she could only tremble at.

'Why?'

It was a thread of sound, but he heard. His head swivelled
towards her. Something darkened in his eyes but he fought it
down, asserting control.

'I heard something,' he said thickly. And obscurely, he
added, 'It wasn't meant to——'

'What?' As she asked the question she heard the sound of a
key in the lock of the outer door, and only one person had a
key.

Peter. Slowly dreadfully, pieces began to fall inexorably into
place. Her eyes burned in the pallor of her face. But even as
she directed a look of panic his way Jake moved. In one swift
movement he thrust her beneath the covers, pulling the sheet
up so that it covered her nakedness, then he sat down on the
side of the bed.

Cathy knew perfectly well what it looked like. Her clothes
were spread on the floor where she had dropped them, her
mouth softly swollen from the passion of his kisses, her eyes
still smoky with the rapidly dwindling passion he had, oh, so
skilfully roused in her. Roused, but not consummated. In a
strange way Jake Ferrers was an honourable man.

A cold, defiant anger shook her slender body, beating back
the pit of sick desolation which gaped beneath. From the
sitting-room there came voices, Peter objecting, Emma

insistent; almost immediately they became louder, progressing towards the bedroom.

Jake's dark profile was slashed from granite as he looked at the two people who appeared as suddenly as puppets in the doorway, his voice implacable. 'Yes?'

Peter looked as sick as Cathy felt. In a voice she had never heard him use before, a new, hard voice, he said, 'This, I regret to say, was Emma's idea. We'll go.'

But Emma was not going to skimp on what she saw as her pound of flesh. White-faced, colour in garish patches on her cheekbones, she made no attempt to hide an intolerable triumph. In a smug, savage voice she said, 'Not feeling well, darling? Didn't you know that your sweet little princess slept with other men?'

'That is enough.' He looked at her as though he had never seen her before, then transferred his gaze to Cathy. She felt Jake's hand clench on her shoulder as Peter drank in the picture she made, small and slender, her hair tumbling in a mass of molten silk around her shoulders, her features betraying only too clearly what had happened before his arrival on the scene. She met his eyes frankly and was astonished and more than a little alarmed at the pain she saw reflected in his.

She said, 'Pete——' and made a movement towards him, but Jake held her in place, exerting his strength to hold her clamped at his side. His hand moved slowly across her shoulder, dark skin against fair, blatantly possessive.

The tense silence was broken shockingly by Emma's laugh. Scanning Cathy's stunned face with bitter pleasure she said, 'You've lost, Cathy, both of them, Jake as well as Peter. Only you never really had Jake, I'm afraid. He's just spent the last boring weeks sweet-talking——'

'That's enough.'

Jake's voice cut the poisonous diatribe off. Emma hesitated, her eyes raking Cathy's closed little face as she swallowed the rest of the corrosive, uncontrolled words. 'Jake?' she said uncertainly. Her eyes searched his face, half ashamed, half pleading. 'But Jake—this is how we planned it. What's wrong?'

He got to his feet, anger a dark force beating through his words. 'Planned what? What the hell are you talking about?'

Emma laughed, and turned her head towards Cathy, but her eyes stayed fixed on the dark mask of Jake's face.

'You see, Cathy, Peter has always thought that deep down you were in love with him. That's because in lots of ways he's rather innocent about women. For some strange reason he even believes that you were still a virgin before you and he started your little affair; I could see that the only way to convince him that you're far from innocent was to discover you in bed with someone else. Fortunately Jake was available.'

Nausea roiled in Cathy's stomach. For the first time in her life she was glad that she had her grandfather's strength, the will which enabled her to reveal nothing of the torment slashing through her body like a death wound. It felt as though her heart had been offered as a sacrifice to the cruellest god of all.

In spite of it all, she said no word, somehow sensing that it was necessary for Emma to rid herself of all the accumulated poisons she had bottled up. Yet Emma was nothing; a greater betrayal was eating into her soul. She didn't look at Jake, but she could feel him and she knew that his whole attention was on his sister.

Emma said now, shrilly, 'Tell her, Jake. Tell her how we set her up so that Peter could see her for the slut she is.'

In a voice she didn't recognise Cathy said, 'Yes, tell me, Jake.'

The eyes which met hers were as chilly as antarctic pack-ice.

Evenly he said, 'I planned no such thing.'

Emma pleaded. 'Yes, you did, Jake. You came to see me this afternoon and told me where you were going and I told you that Peter had a key to her flat and we planned it all . . .' Her voice trailed away. She looked around wildly, then fixed her eyes again on her brother. 'I had to rely on you. There's no one else. Peter is disloyal,' she said, as though explaining something of great importance. 'He doesn't know what she's like. He even made excuses for her when he told me how she and her horrible old grandfather blackmailed Trent Addison into marrying her. I had to act, once and for all, so that he could see her for what she really is, a little slut——'

Jake's voice rang out with sudden sharp authority. 'That's enough!'

Cathy felt a cold dampness on her skin. Her head swam but she saw Peter close his eyes a moment then look directly at her, his expression pleading. 'I'm sorry,' he said in a toneless voice, before, for the first time, looking at his wife. 'Come away,' he said.

'Hadn't you better give Cathy back her key?' Jake suggested.

There was a small clink as Peter dropped it on to the dressing-table. As he walked out Emma burst into speech. 'I don't ever want to see you again! You've done your best to ruin my marriage, just stay out of my life in future. Now that Peter knows what you are, a tramp and a tease, he'll no longer think he's in love with you.'

Bursting into tears, she whirled and followed at a run. Cathy said in a leaden voice, 'Peter has never thought he was in love with me.'

Jake's voice was very level, very hard. 'Don't pretend to be stupid, Cathy, you had him on a string. Do I have your promise to leave him alone?'

She said wearily, 'He's my oldest friend.'

'If I don't get your promise I'll force it from you,' he said silkily.

But she shrugged, because there was nothing more he could do with her, no way he could increase his betrayal. His finger on her chin was an unwelcome intrusion but she allowed him to turn her face so that he could look down into it. She was not afraid of him. She felt no emotion at all, only sadness because that flash of pain in Peter's eyes had convinced her that although Peter was not in love with her he was possessive of her. If he and Emma were to salvage anything from the mess that was their marriage, she would have to leave them alone.

'Give me your promise,' Jake said.

She looked at him without recognition. Then she shrugged again and said indifferently, 'Go to hell.'

His eyes swept her face, very keen and sharp, before he nodded. Cathy heard the hiss of his indrawn breath as he said, 'You believed her.'

She was imprisoned in the shifting patterns of light in his eyes, green turning to blue, to aquamarine, and finally icing to an opaque unreadable enamel. It was as though she had been running over a beach and was suddenly dragged down into quicksands.

A smile curled the straight line of his mouth. He bent his head and kissed her, forcing her head back into the pillow; she shuddered, hating her helplessness, unable to move or breathe as his mouth ravaged hers.

It lasted only a minute. He lifted his head and with a careless hand pushed down the sheet so that he could see her breasts, pale and soft, the tips lifted in an urgency of pleading. That hard smile became tinged with contempt.

'What kind of man do you think I am?' he said as his hand slid across the cool silk of her skin.

She was unable to answer and he demanded, 'Well?'

Suddenly she was exhausted, disillusion tearing the last remnants of her control into shreds.

'Yes, I'll make sure that I don't see Peter again,' she said remotely. 'Will you go, please.'

'That's not what I want to hear, Cathy. Do you believe——?'

A rapid clatter of footsteps announced Emma's reappearance, just, Cathy thought tiredly, like the arrival of a wicked fairy.

Without haste Jake got to his feet, pulling on his shirt with a composure which astounded Cathy. 'What is it?' he asked, almost wearily.

In a voice wavering between anger and fear Emma burst out, 'He just drove off and left me!' She looked around as though she expected to see Peter materialise in the middle of the carpet, then advanced towards the bed, her expression contorting into mindless hate.

'You little bitch!' she spat, girding herself up for more.

In a way Cathy almost welcomed her unbalanced behaviour, it took her mind off the appalling desolation that lay in wait for her just below the surface of her composure. 'I wonder,' she observed calmly, 'how it is that tall women seem to be able to make the word *little* seem like an insult.'

Emma opened her mouth to retaliate; Jake, however, had other ideas. By now fully dressed, he said curtly, 'Stop that, Emma, it's not going to help.'

Emma looked almost demented but she obeyed, turning towards him and bursting into noisy tears. He held her in a protective embrace, his eyes shadowed by the dark brows pulled together in a frown. For a second Cathy wondered whether he was hesitating, unable to decide what to do next.

If it was so it didn't last long. He said quietly, 'Come on, I'll take you home.' He took her arm and without looking again at Cathy led his sister away.

Cathy waited until she heard the door thud behind them before she got up and slid the security lock across. Then she took two sleeping-pills and lay very still reciting the times tables until the drug took effect.

CHAPTER SIX

WHEN her pregnancy was confirmed Melly Addison gave up running in favour of swimming; at this time of year it was no hardship. In fact, she had been relieved to find that a swim as soon as she got up helped alleviate the sickness which had been making her mornings miserable.

This morning she lay back on the lounger and let her eyes wander down the length of her body, trying to assess the changes pregnancy had made. Even as she grimaced her hand ran caressingly over the thickened contours of her waist and her black eyes softened. Soon she would have to buy herself some maternity clothes . . .

A staccato clack of heels lifted her eyes to the corner of the house. Frowning, she watched as Cathy's small, erect figure made its way towards her. Arrogant as ever, she thought wryly as she got to her feet. Dark glasses hid Cathy's eyes, but her first words were delivered in the peremptory tone that Melly always associated with her.

'Is Trent here?'

'No,' Melly said distantly. 'He had to go to work early.'

Cathy's breath sighed out through trembling lips. Since she had woken, headachy and nauseated, she had been buoyed by the irrational conviction that if she could only get to Trent he would know how to deal with the pain which threatened to rip her apart. His absence seemed the greatest betrayal of all. She stood limply, shoulders sagging.

'Oh,' she said in a faraway little voice, and turned to go.

Melly asked quickly, 'Cathy, what is it?'

If she said another word the pain would tear her in two. Cathy's hands clutched protectively at her midriff but she managed to stay almost upright. Behind the protective screen of her glasses her eyes were wide and unseeing.

'Sit down,' Melly ordered in a tone which was meant to be obeyed. When Cathy just fixed her with that terrifying blind stare she came over and took the stiff little body in her arms. 'Cathy, what's happened?' she whispered. 'What is it? Do you want me to ring Trent and get him home?'

Cathy could only manage a choked no, but when Melly urged her towards a chair she obeyed, allowing herself to be put into it. Then she said in that strange, toneless little voice, 'I'm sorry, I shouldn't be here. Only—I've got into the habit of relying on Trent, you see. I know it's been a bore for him and annoying for you, but I think . . .' Her voice trailed away. She looked around vaguely at the cool, lovely garden and made to get to her feet. 'I'm sorry,' she said again as though she couldn't think of anything else to say.

Thoroughly alarmed, Melly put a hand on the slight shoulder and sat her down again. 'You are not going anywhere,' she told her firmly. 'You've had a shock and I'm going to get you some brandy and then you're going to stay here until Trent comes home. He'd never forgive me if I let you go away the way you are now, and I'd never forgive myself. Now, don't move until I come back.'

Lulled by the authentic maternal voice Cathy relaxed. Some people had a talent for motherhood; Melly was clearly one of them. She closed her eyes, wrenched by pain so acute that beads of sweat sprang out over her nose and forehead. The quiet loveliness of the garden was blocked out by a vision of Jake's face as he had seen it last, totally without expression, slicing at her with a hard impersonal stare so absolute that it had cut right through to her bones.

He had chosen to go with Emma rather than stay with her; she didn't know whether he and his sister had conspired together, but there could be no doubt that Emma was more important to him than she was. Cathy thought she would never be able to feel again. When Melly handed her a glass she sat with her fingers curved around it as though seeking warmth.

'Drink it,' Melly commanded.

Obediently Cathy sipped at the foul stuff until it was all gone and she felt a treacherous glow through her body.

'Mrs Jameson is making tea,' Melly told her.

Cathy nodded. Of course. In New Zealand a cup of tea was a necessary accompaniment to all life's dramas. So she waited silently until the housekeeper came through with a tray. Melly poured and Cathy drank that too. In a way it was less painful to do these small actions; they gave her sluggish mind something to seize upon.

She looked over at Melly, tall and still slim in her bikini, her skin glowing, her expression concerned yet basically serene and oh, so happy, and she cried out in anguish, 'I knew I had to be punished, but I thought that working in the orphanage would have helped!'

Melly stared at her in horror. 'What is it? Cathy, who has done this to you?'

A year—a *week*—ago Cathy would never have entertained the idea of telling Melly Addison anything about her innermost feelings. Now she listened as the words tumbled out without volition, almost as though another person was speaking, to finish with a plea about the lesser treachery, 'What's wrong with me? I thought Peter was my friend. I trusted him—why did he tell Emma all about me?'

'Oh, my dear, who knows?' Melly's voice was husky with compassion and understanding. 'Who knows why one person betrays another? Peter is charming but weak.'

Cathy hugged her body. Behind the dark glasses her eyes stung. 'Jake blamed me for that,' she said in a muffled voice.

Melly offered cautiously, 'It sounds as though he has always protected his sister, considered himself responsible for her. He must have felt that she was dangerously close to breaking down . . .' She couldn't go on.

Cathy looked up, her face stretched in a meaningless smile. In a tone that invited derision, she said, 'Whereas everyone knows Cathy Durrant is as tough as old boots, as well as being spoiled and selfish and arrogant. You know, I hoped he might learn to love me. Or at least to want me as much as I want—wanted him. It's been like magic . . . I thought I knew how you and Trent feel about each other, because that's how I felt for him. But it was all a con. What's wrong with me? I love Peter—I thought he was the brother I always wanted. But he found it quite easy to tell my most intimate secrets. And Jake—well, last night couldn't have made it more plain that whatever he feels for me, it's nowhere near as strong as his sense of responsibility towards Emma.' She looked up at Melly, her mouth twisting. 'Perhaps it's a punishment for causing you all that pain. But I didn't know. I swear I didn't know what it's like to love and be hurt . . .'

Melly was out of her chair in a flash, kneeling beside the chair as she took Cathy's shoulders and shook her fiercely. 'You were never vicious, and this idea of punishment is ridiculous! You are not to believe that!'

Cathy drew a deep sobbing breath. 'But if I hadn't blackmailed Trent into marrying me——'

'Listen,' Melly interrupted, suddenly blazing with anger, 'and listen carefully! You married Trent when you were a frightened kid looking for someone to love you, and you chose Trent because you sensed that he was trustworthy as nobody else in your life was. And you were right, weren't you? You found that you had chosen correctly. He is totally trustworthy. Possibly he might have learned to love you if he hadn't already been in love with me. When you discovered what you had done you humbled yourself to come and tell me, and don't think I don't know how much courage that took! We might not have got married if you hadn't done that.'

Cathy shook her head, her mass of hair tumbling like living

silk on to the hands that gripped her shoulders. 'No, that's not so. Trent wanted you, he would never have let you get away from him a second time.'

Releasing her, Melly sat back on her heels, scanning the beaten little face. In a calm, positive voice she stated, 'It would have taken him much longer to persuade me, nevertheless. You short-circuited a lot of fussing about when you came and told me why he had married you. As for this—this latest situation, it has nothing to do with what happened five years ago. You have been messily dragged into someone else's marriage and they should all be damned ashamed of themselves! I'd like to have them here for half an hour!'

Cathy took off her glasses and looked at her. Melly's militant expression altered, became sad and so deeply compassionate that Cathy had to swallow hard to avert the tears which ached at the back of her eyes.

'Oh, Cathy,' she said. 'I know how it feels, love.'

Like a weary child Cathy asked, 'Does it get better?'

'Yes.' Melly got to her feet and said more strongly, 'Yes, it does get better. After a while it fades into the background and you go on living. You even think it's gone. Eventually, I suppose, it does go. And that's the way it should be. You learn from everything that's happened to you, everything you do. Would you like to be the same Cathy Durrant who married Trent five years ago?'

'No. Oh, no!'

'There you are, then.'

Cathy said with a sting, 'You'll excuse me if I can't take the comfort you intend from that just yet, won't you?'

Melly laughed. 'Oh, you've got spirit—I used to envy you that, you know. The air seems to sizzle about you when you move.' She paused, watching Cathy carefully before asking with a soft caution, 'My dear, are you sure that Jake Ferrers isn't in love with you? From what you've said, he——'

'No. Oh, he wants me, but that really doesn't mean much,

does it. I mean—men can want women they don't even like! It doesn't really matter whether or not he planned to have Peter interrupt us last night, because that's not the issue.'

Melly sighed. 'What is the issue, then?'

'I'm greedy, I want more than he can give. He looked at me it was as if I were nothing. Not even the trash Emma thinks I am—just nothing. And when she came back he just took her away as though I didn't exist.' Cathy got to her feet, fighting the pain that bit so deeply into her. In a voice that was still and steady and cold with strain she went on, 'She is clearly more important to him that I am, so he was using me. I despise him.'

'That's the spirit.' Melly certainly appeared convinced, although Cathy could feel her watchful eyes on her. She asked casually, 'What are you planning to do now?'

'I don't know.'

Melly's black curls bobbed about her head as she gave a decisive nod. 'Well, you're going to stay here until you've made up your mind.'

'Oh, no, I can't. I don't really know why I came . . .' A bitter little smile twisted her mouth. 'I suppose I wanted someone to kiss me better. I'm sorry, I wasn't thinking . . . I'll go home.'

But if Cathy was obstinate Melly could be more so, and when Trent came home their reluctant guest was in one of the guest bedrooms sleeping off the after-effects of the sedatives she had taken the night before.

It was quite late when she woke up, disorientated and with her head still pounding, her small body lying in a tight curl in the big bed. She even put out her hand, but when it encountered nothing but emptiness she remembered. A stifled sob broke the heavy silence but it was the only one. Fiercely she refused to give in to the pain. He was not worth one tear. None of them were. In their separate and individual ways they had all betrayed her and she hated them.

For a long time she lay huddled, whipping up her emotions

to cover the desolation that yawned at her feet. At last she got up and padded across to the window. Trent and Melly had built their house on a couple of acres overlooking a big reserve of bush; it was completely private with only the glow of the lights to reveal that they were in the heart of the city. A morepork called from the depths of the bush. There was a silence before he was answered.

It was late, but not, Cathy deduced, after midnight. She wondered if the others were still awake. In the short months of their marriage Trent had never gone to bed before midnight, but then, she thought drily, it had been a cold and lonely bed that awaited him. Now he had Melly. And I *will not* feel envious, she vowed savagely.

It was very quiet, very peaceful, but she stiffened, aware of something alien in the atmosphere. Before she could fathom out what it was that lifted the hairs on the back of her neck, a shadow detached itself from a piece of darkness and in one smooth efficient lunge came in through the open window beside her. Before she had time to scream she was jerked against a hard body and a hand was cutting off her breath as Jake's voice hissed in her ear, 'Shut up, I'm not going to hurt you.'

Her heart thundered in her breast, whether with fear or delight she didn't know. He waited, those cruel fingers clamped across her mouth, then said softly, 'Nod if you're going to co-operate.'

Hastily she nodded. He eased his hand away, lean fingers curled loosely around her throat so that if she screamed he'd be able to cut her breath off again.

'What do you want?'

She could see a flash of white as he told her blandly, 'Merely to find out where Peter is.'

Hope died. 'You could have rung.'

'I did, and was told that you were unable to come to the phone. The second time the fair Mrs Addison told me that it was useless ringing as you didn't want to speak to me.'

'She was right. I've been asleep,' she said.

'Tired. More than understandable. Now, where is Peter?'

Her skin had heated to fire at his casual reference to the night before; now it chilled and she could feel a shiver scour over her skin. 'I don't know,' she said flatly.

'Sure? I can think of several interesting ways to jog your memory.'

The threat was delivered in an off-hand tone but the shiver became a full-fledged shudder. 'No. Do you think I'd be likely to keep tabs on him after learning what he did?'

The deep voice was smooth and ironical.

'Unforgiving little soul, aren't you. Some people are unable to keep secrets in bed, you know.'

'Treachery,' she returned through her teeth, 'is the one unforgivable sin. Now, will you go? I don't know how efficient Trent's security is, but I wouldn't push your luck too far.'

'If it's been triggered he'd have been here before now.' A note of recklessness in the cool voice told her that he had probably enjoyed outwitting Trent's system.

Exasperation at such a peculiarly masculine attitude was eclipsed by another, more primitive emotion as he said in a voice of rough velvet, 'I also came to tell you that I hadn't planned to set you up last night. The whole idea was Emma's.'

She shrugged, and he said sharply, 'Do you understand?'

'Perfectly.' The word whispered through the air. 'Yes, I understand. I just don't care any more, Jake. You've done what I presume you set out to do, you've convinced Emma that she has nothing to fear from me. Just go.' Her weary distaste was evident in her voice. She felt sickened and smirched by the whole affair.

His fingers touched the cool hollow at the base of her throat, resting for a long moment on the small throbbing pulse, as though testing for her reaction. In a voice that was even and devoid of emotion he said, 'Emma is perilously close to a nervous breakdown.'

'I could see that for myself.'

'Yet neither you nor Peter gave her the reassurance she needs so much.' The condemnation was infused with contempt.

Tension spun a ragged thread through her reply. 'I think Peter tried. I'm afraid I was branded the enemy. Anything I said was immediately assumed to be a lie. I feel sorry for her, and sorry for you, because it's clear that you are going to spend the rest of your life trying to keep her on an even keel.'

'Is that why you're so angry? Because I left your bed to take my sick sister home?'

Put like that—yet she knew, none better, that attack was sometimes the only way to defend an indefensible position. She said quietly, 'No. I'm glad you went, it gave me time to come to my senses. Please go, Jake. For what it's worth, I don't know where Peter is.'

'Are you sure? You haven't decided on a place where you'll meet him in a few days, have you?'

Distaste sharpened the words as she replied, 'No. From now on I am not interested in anything Peter does, or anything you or Emma do. You can settle your own affairs without my help.'

His chuckle was silent yet she was standing so close to him that she could feel the rise and fall of his chest. 'Have I broken the mould?' he asked softly. 'Always before you've managed to keep your lovers as friends, haven't you.'

She said in an empty voice, 'You are not my lover. Will you go, please. I don't ever want to see you again.'

'An entirely mutual desire,' he said, but something in his tone brought her stiffly upright, her incredulous eyes lifting to the hard silhouette above her.

She could see him better now, the strongly hewn features emphasised even more forcefully by the shadows. She could discern the arrogant line of nose and jaw, sweep of cheekbone and breadth of brow, and in the darkness below those brows his narrowed eyes burned in a stare she recognised, fixed on to the smooth outlines of her mouth.

She whispered, 'No!' but if the word made it through her lips that was all that did. His mouth closed on hers with the urgency of a predator about to satisfy its hunger after a long starvation; he used his thumb to push up her chin so that her mouth and throat were exposed to him in the classic gesture of submission as he took his fill of the sweetness of her mouth.

It was ravishment and anguish and ecstasy, the sensual perfection totally overwhelming the cool processes of her brain. Shivering, she sensed the barely restrained violence in him and was afraid of it, yet something in her responded with a like fierceness so that her hands clenched around his back as she pulled herself against him.

Logic, reason, common sense—all fled before the relentless force of the passions they aroused in each other, like calling to like in an explosion of uncontrollable need. His mouth sought hers in kisses which blazed like bonfires; once he said her name in a deep gasping moan, his hands unconsciously cruel on her small body, and she whispered a reply, a plea, a demand—later, she couldn't even remember what words had tumbled from her heated lips.

He kissed her again and his hands pulled at the material of her top, sliding beneath the cotton to palm her breast; a deep, involuntary breath lifted the wall of his chest as the bud of her nipple peaked in his hand, a silent, potent invitation.

Cathy was kissing his throat, her small teeth grazing the skin; an agony of need burned through her body, searing away the resentment and heartbreak of the day. The very intensity of her emotions, the pain and the anger, joined with her purely physical response so that she was witless and shaking, all female, all hunger.

And beneath it all, adding to it, was a love as wild as the tempest, primeval and basic, without inhibitions or shame.

'Cathy,' he whispered, his body rigid with desire as he

hauled her against him in a movement so blatantly sexual that she felt her nervous system scream into overload. 'Cathy, I need you.'

She closed her eyes at the pagan glitter of his, scorched by the message she read there. He was moving against her, causing such sensations that a half-choked little moan thrilled through her; she thought dazedly that she had never known that a man's body could be so incredibly exciting, create such chaos in the orderly processes of her own.

At that moment she could have lain down beneath him on the hard stone of the terrace, careless of anything but the driving need to assuage the fires he had lit in her.

And then he said in thick, defeated voice, 'My God, not here!' and tore her arms from around his neck, almost throwing her against the railing. She landed in a little huddled heap, her whole body so bereft that she almost cried out with the shock of it.

He said roughly, 'Just leave Peter alone. Give them the chance to get their marriage on an even keel.'

So he still believed her to have been Peter's lover. She couldn't answer, couldn't move her tongue in her dry mouth. Numbly, she watched as he turned and strode across the lawn.

No sooner had his silent presence faded into the deeper shadows of the trees than she saw another figure come around the corner of the house.

'Trent,' she whispered. 'How long have you——?'

He asked calmly, 'Are you all right?'

'Yes.'

'I haven't been eavesdropping.'

'How did you know he was here?'

'I have,' he said grimly, 'a very good security system. I knew as soon as he came over the fence. I didn't interrupt because I thought you might like the chance to talk to him. Melly is convinced that you don't want to see him, but the man deserves a chance to put his side of things.'

She said hopelessly, 'He came to ask where Pete was. I gather he's left Emma. I don't think he believed me when I said I didn't know where he was. Trent, I have to go away. I'm not—I can't——'

He said something beneath his breath and looped an arm about her shoulder, turning her into the room. 'It will be better in the morning,' he said.

But the morning brought Emma, half hysterical, screaming threats and abuse at Cathy until she had her face slapped by an extremely angry Melly.

'That will do,' she said icily. 'I don't care how you behave in your own home, but in this house you can try for some sort of control. You are not welcome here. Stop harassing Cathy or I'll call the police in.'

Holding her hand to her smarting cheek, Emma drew a deep breath, but something in Melly's face brought her up short. She muttered sullenly, 'I just want to know where Peter is.'

'If this is any indication of how you behave with him I'd say he's running as fast and as far as he can,' Melly said acidly. 'Men can't stand hysterics.'

'*She* knows,' Emma sneered. 'Little whore.'

Melly lifted her brows, her distaste obvious. 'What a commonplace little mind you have,' she said calmly. 'Are you sure you are in a fit state to drive home?' She looked up and said in exactly the same voice, 'Ah, Jake. Emma is just going home. If you have any affection for her, try to convince her that she is only making a fool of herself.'

He looked dangerous and grim, his expression as black as thunder. It did not relax even when Emma flung herself with a burst of loud sobs on his chest. One hand came around to keep her still; he looked at Melly and said, 'I'm sorry, it won't happen again. Come on, Emma, I'll take you home.'

Cathy moved her head the merest fraction but he still didn't look at her. He had not looked at her at all. He took his sister away and she watched them go, believing in the depths of her frozen heart that this was the last time she would see him.

A snatch of an old prayer, one of the psalms, came into her head. *Deliver my soul from the sword: my darling from the power of the dog.*

She had always shuddered at the barbaric picture it evoked, redolent of ancient cruelties. Now she knew what it meant.

Crisply Melly said, 'What a stupid girl. If that's the preliminary to a breakdown it appears to have a strong scent of calculation to me! No wonder Peter ran away if she treats him to a circus like that every time he annoys her. Now, I'll make us a cup of coffee . . .'

The bell of the telephone interrupted; she threw a concerned look at Cathy's still figure and went off to answer it. When she came back Cathy hadn't moved. She was standing looking at her hands as if she had never seen such things before.

The sound of Melly's voice brought her head up. 'How would you like to stay with my brother and his wife at their station up north?' Cathy heard her say.

'I don't know them.'

'Yes, you do, you went to their wedding. Rafe and Jennet Hollingworth, remember?'

Cathy looked at her. 'Who was on the telephone?'

'You always were too sharp for your own good,' Melly said calmly. 'About my brother——'

'I'm not a child. An idiot, perhaps, but not a child. Who was on the phone?'

Melly sent her a sharp look then shrugged. 'A journalist. Apparently Emma has been talking all around town.'

'About what?' When Melly hesitated Cathy said dully, 'About how I "persuaded" Trent to marry me, I suppose. Oh God, Melly, I'm sorry. I'm so sorry.'

'I know you're sorry, and wallowing in self-pity is not going to help the situation. Now, about Rafe and Jen——'

Cathy was looking at her but she did not see her. Slowly, almost hesitantly, she said, 'I've run away enough. I'm not

going to do it any more. All my life I've run away. It's time I
stopped. Thank you for trying to make things easier for me,
but it seems to me it's about time I stood up for myself. I used
to want to be like my grandmother because she was kind and
she loved me, but she was weak. When it came to the crunch
she couldn't stand against my grandfather.'

Melly looked at her with surprise, and then alarm. The
intense little face was white yet peculiarly alert; a frown
narrowed the space between the thin brows.

'I've always been powerless,' Cathy said, thinking fiercely.
'And useless. Other people manage my life and I've just let
them. The only time I took control of my own affairs was
when I forced Trent to marry me, and you know how that
turned out. But if you are powerless you get exploited. You ask
to be exploited.' She finished slowly, 'I am sick of being weak.'

Melly said cautiously, 'So?'

But Cathy was not ready to admit what she was feeling. The
tension faded from her features; she replied in a remote voice,
'So I have a lot of thinking to do.'

'Where do you plan to do it?'

She said guardedly, 'Back on the island. I doubt if anyone
will track me down to there. I won't answer the telephone.'

'You will at eight-thirty each morning,' Melly insisted, and
wouldn't give up until Cathy agreed. A few hours later she left
the sanctuary of Trent's house in his helicopter, and on the
way across the harbour and Gulf she pondered on the fact that
she had at last found common ground with Melly. She had
always thought Peter her one true friend; now, she wondered
whether perhaps, in the years to come, she and Melly might
become friends too. Her mother was fond of saying that one
woman could never be friends with another, but Cathy
thought now that in that, as in everything else, her mother was
too much of a cynic.

Once back on the island, she warned the Stallworthys that
officially she was not in residence and was careful not to

answer the telephone except for the one call at eight-thirty each morning; she spent the rest of the time trying valiantly to put her life together. Common sense told her that regrets and recriminations were useless, but it was easier to believe the precept than to actually follow it.

The sun stretched out the days into summer, gold and green and blue, warm and somnolent as only summer can be. The Gulf took on its busy aspect, silver in the early mornings, streaked by the trails of yachts and powerboats, the sky riding high above the shimmering plane of the sea and the smooth, sharp contours of the land. At night the stars scintillated down, clear and sharp as diamonds in the warm air, more brilliant than she had ever seen them before.

Or perhaps it was that she saw much more of them. Sleep did not come easily, and she sat out on the terrace often, watching those stars, listening to the harsh cries of the kiwi family in the bush behind the bay, and thinking rather ironically of the Maori woman of long ago who had loved and been betrayed.

No doubt her anguish had been as real and as painful as this sensation which was tearing Cathy in two. At least, she thought one particularly bad night, that woman of long ago had not had to endure it for long.

The days ahead spread out before her, long and grey and endless as infinity, filled with dreary trivialities. She put her face in her hands and wept.

The bout left her exhausted, with a headache which was still nagging the next morning. To try to get rid of it she went for a walk along the beach, unconsciously following the path towards the glow-worm bank; with grim humour she thought it was rather like the impulse that urged her to swallow continually when she had a bad bout of tonsillitis.

She was not brave enough to go the whole way. Without really making the decision she struck away from the beach and climbed the steep hillside to the ramparts of the old *pa*, arriving at the top scarlet and weary, her breath coming harshly from her lungs. Alarmed sheep scattered, but when she collapsed on to the short prickly grass they reformed and began again on their endless task of converting grass to wool. Except for a few lambs who found a small knoll and with the brisk cheerfulness of their sort began playing follow-my-leader down it.

Cathy looked away, seeking solace in the view. From up there the island was small, the smoky-blue bush covering more than half of its area. She looked blindly out, drawing a deep, sobbing breath as the colour of the sea merged into aquamarine eyes, cold and cutting, despising her even as they blazed with desire.

That was something that Emma could not take away. In spite of everything, Jake had wanted her, Cathy. She thought wearily that it was little enough to cherish, that casual lust, but it seemed that it was all she was ever going to have.

She had spent her life terrified of rejection, yet something about her attracted it, as if she had a fatal flaw.

'No,' she said fiercely, striking a clenched fist on the soft grass. She would not admit that. Bad luck, perhaps, and some of it had been her own fault, but at least she was learning.

Rolling over on to her stomach, she lay frowning down at the wide sweep of sea and land. There were millions of others in the world who were infinitely worse off than she, thousands of them even in this beloved country of hers. Children such as those she had cared for at the orphanage; children in cities who never had the chance to enjoy the sort of view before her now.

She thought of her grandmother who had loved children and worked for them all her life in the only way she knew how, heading charity committees and organising fund-raising. Such help had been needed, but her methods were not for Cathy . . .

Her eyes narrowed, became focused on the bay beneath. A grassy wedge of land, about ten acres, backed a wide white crescent of sand. There were pohutukawa trees and the beach shelved gently. After a few moments the kernel of an idea took over and she began to look very like her grandfather when he plotted some new coup.

That night she rang Trent. After preliminaries she said crisply, 'Trent, I want to turn part of the island over to a trust.'

He sounded amused. 'Do you, indeed. Why?'

'I want to set up an adventure camp for children. At first I thought it should be just for underprivileged children, but that didn't seem fair, so I think it should be for all. I'd like to use my grandmother's money to set it up, provide the buildings and so on, and then we'd need to set up a trust fund to keep it going. In memory of my grandmother. And Sir Peter, I suppose.'

Trent laughed. 'I doubt,' he said drily, 'whether he'd thank you for that. He's probably turning in his grave at the thought of you giving away his hard-earned money.'

'My grandmother's money was not his.'

'No.' He thought for some moments. 'Are you sure you want to do this?'

'Yes, I do. I've actually been thinking of doing something with her money ever since I came back. I don't need it. In a way, it's sinful to have as much as I've got without earning any of it.'

'Noble of you,' he said drily.

She said with something of a snap, 'I can afford a little nobility, surely!'

'A considerable amount,' he agreed, not in the least impressed.

She gave a reluctant chuckle. 'Would it add unbearably to your job as one of my trustees if I went ahead with it?'

'Yes. However, I can see no reason why you shouldn't do a fair amount of the work.'

She was startled at the idea, but the more she thought of it the more she liked it. At the very least it would take her mind off her own woes, perhaps even ease this bitter ache which seemed located in the marrow of her bones.

She had not known that unhappiness was a physical pain. It had never occurred to her that it could throb through her body until she felt as ill as she had with the tropical disease which had brought her out of the jungle.

And she had not known that frustration was a taste in the mouth, love unrequited an agony of regret and anger. But not despair. She refused to allow herself that dangerous luxury. She told herself very sternly that others had survived broken hearts, and so would she.

CHAPTER SEVEN

AFTER a lonely Christmas spent, in spite of Melly's entreaties, with the Stallworthys, Cathy plucked up enough courage to ask whether Jake was still in Auckland.

'He was here until after Christmas,' Melly said, 'but I hear that he's gone back home.'

Where, her tone implied, I hope he gets frostbite, at the very least.

'I see.' Cathy realised she was chewing on her lip and hastily stopped.

'Emma has had what is tactfully called a breakdown. She is, however, still with Peter.'

Which sounded hopeful. 'Ah—I think I might come home.'

Melly said dolefully, 'It's incredibly humid here, everyone who is able to has fled to the beach. New Zealand is taking its annual holiday.'

'Poor Melly, are you suffering badly? Why doesn't Trent send you up north to your brother's?'

'Don't you start, too. Trent has to be in Auckland, and so I want to be here.'

'Lucky Trent,' Cathy said softly.

Melly said nothing for a moment, then gave a surprised laugh. 'Well, I happen to think I'm incredibly lucky too. And I spend most of the day in the pool, so I'm not finding it too bad. When do you intend to come back?'

'Tomorrow.'

But the next day brought a shock with it. As always Cathy woke very early, almost as the sun came up, and as always she slipped from the house to go down to the beach, her robe over her arm. The dew hung heavily on the grass, slapping at her legs, trapping the spider webs in arcs of crystal. It was very quiet. Even the gulls were asleep. The air had that indescribably fresh smell of dawn and the sea was still and faintly misty so that a yacht slipping along a mile or so offshore seemed to be only a ghost sail with no hull beneath.

But it was not this that stopped Cathy short at the top of the bank, her eyes fixed with a kind of outrage on the sleek cabin cruiser which lay snug inside the reef, silent and still on the anchor rope.

Although she owned riparian rights they extended only to low-water mark, so whoever had brought the cruiser in through the rocks was perfectly within their rights, but so few people dared the narrow channel that Cathy had always thought of the little bay as her own special preserve.

She felt almost violated. For a moment her fierce gaze fixed on to the white hull as if she would burn a hole right through it, until with a shrug she turned away to walk along to the next bay.

Although the soft sand was cool and damp on her feet, dragging at her calf muscles, she didn't notice. Her head was carefully turned away from the sea while anger burned slow and hot within her. It seemed the final straw that on her last day she should have to suffer an intruder in the bay.

Once on the track she broke into a run, forcing herself to forget the cruiser, forget everything but the quiet morning and the heat of the sun as it burned on to her skin. Just before the next beach she dropped over the bank, wincing slightly as her feet landed on the tough red rocks. She picked her careful way down the low cliff until she arrived once more on sand. Spread before her was the tiny hidden beach that she and Peter had christened the Pirate cove and which had figured largely in their most exciting games.

It had, she thought as she looked about, grown smaller over the years, but was still the same secluded little crescent of sand. Unless it was a very small dinghy or canoe no boat could thread in through the ramparts of reefs, and shielded by the pohutukawas and the cliff face she could not be seen by anyone from above.

Here she was perfectly safe.

The water made her shiver, but a few minutes' energetic swimming soon had the blood coursing vigorously through her veins. However, even here she was not safe from memories.

'Damn you!' she whispered fiercely as she stroked for the shore. 'Get out of my brain!'

How could she forget him when all it took was the colour of the sea to bring the memories back? How could she ever forget?

Well, she could do something to exorcise the memory. With furious strokes she made across to the rocks, pulling herself up in one easy motion. She wore a bikini, old and past its best. Two angry movements stripped the wet material from her body; she dropped them and without looking about her dived into the water.

The water flowed freely over her body, smooth and sensuous like liquid silk, not quite erotic but heightening every sensation. Cathy gave herself up to enjoyment, carefully blanking out the torment of her thoughts.

But even then, in some dark recess of her brain she knew that she had this to thank Jake for. Until she met him she had not known the simple excitement and pleasure that her body was capable of.

Perhaps she would have been better off not knowing, for with this reluctant admission came a vision of him as he had been in her arms, like a god from the barbaric past, frightening, even awe-inspiring in his virile masculinity, yet not swathed in any more mystery than the secrets of his maleness.

And with that vision came the fierce clutch of desire through her body.

Perhaps one day she would be able to thank him for his

gift to her, this new ability to lose herself in sensation. But that day would be a long time coming, and until then she would have to sublimate her grief and pain in anger and work.

It was anger which gave her arms the strength to haul her body through the water with a speed she had probably never attained before, anger and pain which gave her legs the energy to kick; she banished the intrusive memories by concentrating on what she remembered from her swimming-lessons as a child. By trying hard she could even recall her coach's voice.

It was in a depleted, almost exhausted state that she pulled herself out of the water and bent to pick up the bikini pieces. Her hair hung full and heavy across her face. With an impatient gesture she pushed it back, and looked straight up into Jake's dark face.

Panic imposed her reaction. On a stifled scream she whirled and dived into the water.

A moment later she was fighting madly, wrestling with all of her strength beneath the water in a mad tangle of arms and legs which didn't stop until he hauled her up to the surface and shook her, his eyes blazing with anger and some other, starker emotion.

'Stop it!' he said between his teeth. 'Stop it, damn you——' His hand slapped her cheek, not hard but with enough force to stifle hysteria.

She sobbed and went limp, sagging into the water, her flare of energy evaporated. A moment later one hand crept up to her stinging cheek.

'Why did you do that?' she croaked.

He was able to stand on the bottom. His arm tightened about her, holding her upright, just off balance. 'You were about to launch into a full-blown hysterical attack,' he said briefly.

She closed her eyes, because she could see marks on his shoulder, a semi-circle of brutal bruises where her teeth had closed in her panicky resistance.

In a distant little voice she said, 'Clearly you're used to dealing with them. I'm sorry, you frightened me. Let me go, please. *Jake!*'

Because he hoisted her sleek wet body into her arms and was striding towards the shore. Once more panic ran like a black flood through her body. She risked a look and saw a face entirely engraved in stone, the features stark and cruel and cold as ice.

And she fought the panic and subdued it, holding herself rigid in his grasp, her small body stiff and unwelcoming.

On shore he put her down and watched with those curiously opaque eyes as she huddled into her robe, leaving the belt loose because that way the hem came just below the juncture of her thighs. Her chin lifted; she demanded coldly, 'Why are you here?'

He smiled, the set mirthless smile of a man who is determined on having his way. 'I came to collect,' he informed her.

She stiffened. 'You've already had your pound of flesh.'

'Oh, no, I haven't. And I've discovered that I want it. All of it. That last night—you promised me everything. I've come to collect my prize.'

Shaken, almost sickened by his reasonable tone she watched fascinated the tiny muscle flicking beside his mouth. This was danger, stark and terrifying. She said slowly, 'You must be crazy if you think that I——'

'Crazy? Perhaps, but so are you. Because you want it too.'

She opened her mouth to protest but he smothered the words stillborn, taking them from her mouth in a kiss that deepened and intensified until the flames he kindled swept through her brain, obliterating everything but the forbidden hunger smouldering beneath the anger and the hurt pride.

Later she would wonder if it was the pride and the anger which gave an edge to the devouring passion between them, for he too was angry, she could sense it, and the leaping response which seared along her nerves seemed based on an emotion so fierce it couldn't be desire or the love she thought she knew.

This was primitive, a power too furious to be caged by the civilised restraints of real life. Head flung back, she welcomed the forceful invasion of his tongue, her hands gripping the wet polished skin of his shoulders.

He lifted his head, blind hunger glittering in his eyes, skin drawn tightly over the stark framework of his features and hot colour rising behind the bronze as his mouth followed the line of her throat, burning a path to the soft curve of her breasts.

Cathy's breath was trapped in her chest. Helplessly she looked down at the fleshless profile against her skin, dark against pale cream, his mouth wreaking such erotic havoc that she was making strange little noises in her throat. The sun kindled subtle licks of flame in his hair; for the first time she realised that it was not completely black.

Like the man whose head it covered, she thought, her last coherent thought for what seemed hours.

He lifted his head again and smiled, and looked around. Beneath the rocks was a small patch of sand, completely sheltered from the view of anybody at sea or on the land; holding her in a grip as relentless as death he strode over and set her on her feet.

Cathy said, 'I don't——'

'Hush,' he said, and such was his power over her that she was quiet. The sand was warm and soft against her sensitised feet; she stood still as his hands pulled at the sleeves of her robe, slipping them down, pulling the garment free, spreading it out on the sand with a flick of his wrist.

Then he stood looking down at her, watching the way the sun gilded her body, the faint, evanescent shadows of the water on the skin of her breasts and body.

'Eternal woman,' he said softly. 'Enchanting and mysterious, a trap and a haven, heaven and hell blended together in the form of beauty.'

She shivered, because she knew that it was a valediction. He would do this, make her his, and then he would leave her. And she would never see him again.

Perhaps she should have said no. Although he seemed driven by forces beyond control she knew that he would stop if she wanted him to. Her eyes fell on the mark of her teeth on her bare shoulder. The bruise was beginning to show beneath the smooth swell of muscle, and in one spot there was a tiny drop of blood.

My mark, she thought in a strange kind of exultation. I have marked him and although he doesn't know it, he is mine for ever.

And in that moment her mind was made up. With a faint smile she surrendered to the tides that were coursing through her body, surrendered to love.

Her eyes drifted down his torso, avidly, openly appreciating the smooth power of it, a splendid combination of muscles beneath skin as fine and as smooth as oiled silk, bronzed over a bone structure which set him apart from other men.

The alpha male, she thought almost dazedly. Primal instincts stirred, so that the sharp heat of desire was rekindled in the pit of her stomach.

He was wearing shorts, old, faded denims which set off the symmetry and self-contained male beauty of his body. She reached out, and as though he had been waiting for some signal he pulled her close into him, holding her a long moment with his head buried in the place where her neck met her shoulder.

It was not the first time she had felt an aroused male against her, but always before Jake her reaction had been one of distaste. Now she was excited, the hard promise of his masculinity stirring her innermost feelings so that she gasped and pressed against him.

Slowly, almost reluctantly, he released her, to sink on his

knees before her. She shuddered at the feel of his mouth on her waist, the soft skin of her stomach, exploring the hollow of her navel with an eroticism which was all the more potent because it was so controlled. Against her his face was burning, but his mouth moved with exquisitely delicate precision as his arms tightened about her.

Needles of fire ran up through her body. Abruptly, her knees sagged and he gave a triumphant smile and pulled her gently down into his arms. Somewhere up the hill a sheep called; it was answered by the piercing cry of a stilt. Cathy looked up into the dark, intent face above her and sighed deeply, sinking down on to the soft towelling, her small body quivering with unknown sensations, unfulfilled hungers.

It was like no fantasy conjured by her guilty imagination just before sleep. He was gentle, and tormentingly patient, and when she arched against him he was fierce and masterful, demanding without words that she respond to the caress of his hands, his mouth. Of course he made no allowance for her virginity, but even so he knew exactly how to woo her until she was sobbing with frustration, her glazed eyes wild under the experienced ministrations of his fingers and mouth, the slow, merciless building of passion until she too became bold, stripping him with the quick movements of the experienced woman he thought her, touching him as he touched her, discovering the violently pleasurable sensations incurred when skin is stroked with open mouth and knowledgeable, tormenting skill.

Love made her provocative; love rendered her strong, and it was love and a need so overwhelming which brought her finally to the edge of incoherence, her small fists clenched on to his waist as she tried to guide him into the place that ached and stung in need for his weight and his power.

'What do you want?' He spoke almost gutturally, his narrowed eyes almost black in a face slicked with sweat.

'You,' she whispered.

'Say my name.'

'Jake.' She whispered it, and then she shouted it, and groaned it as he laughed and possessed himself of all of her pliant, willing femininity, driving home with a powerful urgency which brought a broken sound to the back of her throat.

But her body accepted his with a smooth tightness, without pain, and when she looked up there was no shock of comprehension in the eyes which burned down into hers. Dusky colour swept along the high arcs of his cheeks; his mouth was a hard line, he looked a man taken out of himself to some sensual realm where passion was as cruel a taskmaster as any slave-owner in far-off times.

Cathy whispered his name, and he began to move, reinforcing his demands, carrying her into that realm of the senses where nothing meant anything but the fire in her blood and the ache deep inside, in the place she almost managed to reach.

And then at last she did reach it and shot over the edge of the world, lost to anything but the exquisite sensations shuddering through her so that although she sobbed out his name over and over again, she was unaware of what she was doing, conscious only that he too had reached that place, and that his body was now slack, all that proud male magnificence hers alone. For the moment.

She turned her head and covered the mark she had made on his shoulder with her mouth. For long moments they lay together, and then, when she had begun to wonder whether he had gone to sleep, he levered himself off her and rolled over on to his back.

Cathy felt his rejection as surely as if he had put it into words. This delicious lassitude would be followed by pain of an intensity she had never before experienced, but she made no attempt to get up, lying with the sun making tiny rainbows at the ends of her lashes.

She braced herself, but instead of leaving he slid an arm

beneath her shoulders and held her against the sunlit warmth of his body, his mouth touching her forehead in an embrace that thrilled her with its tenderness. His free hand roved through the wet red silk of her hair, gently separating out the tangles, then over the curves and hollows of her body, as though using those knowledgeable fingers to imprint the feel of her on to his mind for ever.

For the first time in her life Cathy knew what it was like to lie sheltered by protective arms, with the salt scent of male in her nostrils, the rough support of his chest beneath her cheek. Happiness was a silken cloak, wrapping her in its folds to keep the real world at bay.

Then he got to his feet, saying, 'You have the talent of Delilah. But I knew you would. How many men has it taken to hone your natural skills to that peak of perfection, Cathy?'

Pain. Like a hammer-blow to her heart. Yet she knew what he was doing; she even knew why. Because she too was awed and shaken, more than a little afraid at what had just happened between them. It felt as though someone else had taken over the responses of her body, a desperate uncontrolled stranger with needs and desires so powerful that she had no control over them.

Even as the thought passed through her mind she rejected it. Both had known what they were doing, both had their reasons for such a wholesale surrender to passion. She loved him, and she yearned to know the fulfilment of her love.

And he? A desire to purge himself of this inconvenient passion, perhaps. Certainly not love.

His shadow transmuted the dazzle in her eyes into darkness as he stooped to pick up his shorts. She refused to move, a desperate hope flickering for a moment in her heart, then dying out as he moved away.

'Cathy?' The word was peremptory in tone, and was repeated when she made no answer.

Wearily she opened her eyes. He was standing looking down

at her, his face shuttered. 'Oh, go away,' she said tiredly. 'You've got what you wanted, now leave me alone.'

His mouth tightened into a forbidding line but he said nothing, merely turned away and strode out of sight.

After a long time Cathy got to her feet and went back into the water, swimming with mindless vigour until, exhausted, she walked ashore with bowed head.

Mrs Stallworthy was waiting back at the house, her kind face anxious. 'I was just about to come looking for you,' she scolded. 'Jake said that you wouldn't be long.'

'Did he?' Cathy strove to banish the listlessness from her tone.

'Yes. Wasn't it kind of him to come to say goodbye to us all? He's flying back to England tomorrow, he said. Cathy, you've gone and got sunburned, you silly girl! Go inside and put some cream on this minute.'

So she did, after she had used up all the hot water showering. Then she climbed on to her bed and spent the rest of the day there, shivering.

Just today, she promised herself. Tomorrow I'll start to forget him.

It wasn't easy. She waited until she was sure that the jet had left from Mangere airport and then went back to Auckland, a small, erect girl with shadows in her blue eyes and a mouth held too firmly to curve into its usual sultry shape. Once back in the real world she lost no time in putting into effect all the decisions she had made in the dark hours.

The apartment went first. She bought herself a small house in one of the quietest streets in a green suburb, and in between attending the innumerable meetings needed to set the Trust in motion she set about furnishing it. As Melly had warned her, Auckland was hot and humid and almost empty, but she went about her work with a gritty determination which reminded those who came in contact with her of Sir Peter at his more amiable.

Within a few weeks she knew that she was not pregnant and a weight rolled off her heart. She would have had Jake's baby and loved it with all her heart, but sooner or later he would have heard about it and she did not think she could bear to see him again.

She heard nothing from Peter and made no attempt to contact him; she bore him no ill will, for beside Jake's behaviour Peter's seemed the lesser treason. He and Emma would have to work out their own destinies; she hoped that Jake too now understood that.

One day she went up to the museum to admire a collection of South American gold artefacts and met a woman called Alex Severn who had been a prefect at school when Cathy was a third-former.

After the initial greetings, Cathy asked, 'What are you doing here? I thought you lived on an island somewhere up north.'

Alex's beautiful eyes clouded. 'Oh, my parents separated and that life is long over. I'm down here trying to find a cheap flat suitable for a poverty-stricken university student.'

'What are you doing?'

'Maths.' She grinned. 'And a little English Lit. for light relief. And yes, my mother has told me often that maths is totally unfeminine, but I've always been good at it.'

This, as Cathy found out later, was modesty taken to extremes. Brilliant Alex was a graduate student with a fiercely independent streak, struggling through a Master's degree on negligible funds.

'I've become accustomed to penury,' she confided airily over a cup of coffee.

Cathy said slowly, 'I've just bought a house, and I need someone to share it with me. Would you like to?'

'Why?'

Cathy's mouth moved in a self-derisory grin. 'Because I like you. And because I've been crossed in love and if I don't have someone around to keep my mind off myself I might just cut my throat.'

'I see.' And perhaps Alex did, because after another sharp survey she nodded decisively. 'Right, it's a deal, but I pay my own way.'

They surprised the other patrons at the coffee bar by solemnly shaking hands, then exchanging smiles.

Cathy had never had a woman friend before and she found it a pleasant experience. Alex was fun, she worked harder than anyone Cathy had ever known, and she did not pry or throw moods or leave hairs in the handbasin.

It was a busy year. The degree course Cathy had chosen kept her at full stretch intellectually, and any spare time she had was taken over by the endless details involved in setting up the Trust. She had very little time to pine, very little time to wonder what Jake was doing now, and practically no time or desire to go out.

What little socialising she did was mostly under Melly's wing; she and Trent's wife were approaching friendship cautiously, without the misconceptions which had scarred their attitudes before, and Cathy was one of the first to admire the Addisons' new baby when she arrived on the scene, large and red-faced and vigorous, with her mother's black eyes and curly hair.

Only once did Cathy wonder what Jake's child would look like. Repressing the thought as morbid she learned how to knit and presented Louise Melissa with a pair of bright red and white striped bootees and a matching bonnet.

'Gorgeous.' Melly laughed and untied the ribbon from around her daughter's chubby chin. 'I love them.' She crooned a few words to the baby until she obediently went to sleep, then turned perceptive eyes on to her visitor. 'You still look a little fine-drawn. Got over him yet?'

'Of course I have.' Even to Cathy the words sounded a little lacking in conviction. She went on to qualify, 'Well, almost.'

'Hard work, isn't it?' Melly's voice was drily sympathetic.

'But it's worth it in the long run.'

No doubt. Sometimes during that interminable winter Cathy wondered if anything was worth it. She had thought that she had experienced the depths of pain after they had made love, but that had been nothing compared with the ache which seemed an ever-present factor in her life now. Somehow Jake had managed to take all the flavour from her life, and nothing, not the Trust, not the hard work she put in at university, not even the friendship she cherished with Alex and Melly, helped.

And at night, in the moments before sleep when her guard was relaxed, the memories came flooding back. So clearly her treacherous mind recalled his rare gentleness, the intoxicating swiftness of his mind, and what at the time had seemed his genuine liking for her.

But there was the other memory which could not be banished either, the swift desire, his potent virility and fierce, uncompromising strength, and beneath the blankets her body would move restlessly, aching for that surcease from hunger only he could bring her.

Such weakness made her despise herself for wanting a man who had seen her only as an obstacle to his sister's happiness, one he set about removing as quickly and efficiently as possible. But, as she was learning, love knows no pride.

As the months wound their wet way through the winter she grew thinner, more fine-drawn, until she caught Alex looking anxiously at her whenever she pushed a meal away.

Then she said *Enough!* And slowly, with infinitesimal steps forward and many slips backward, she began to pull herself out of the grey world she inhabited. It was difficult, more difficult than anything she had ever done before, but she had strength and pride and determination, and she was not going to pine away from love like some witless Victorian maiden.

She began going out again, not often and always in a group, taking up her social life among the university crowd. They were cheerful and irreverent and they didn't ask questions. Then came the exams and she, like everyone else, developed shadows under her eyes from too much study and not enough sleep. At Christmas she and Alex went across to the island and spent most of their time with the first group of children at the camp, boys and girls from a children's home. It was noisy and special, hot and tiring and filled with moments of emotion, and Cathy came back to Auckland convinced that it had all been worth-while.

Alex went back to her work at a restaurant and for the rest of the summer break Cathy immersed herself in the final details left over from the setting up of the Trust. She co-opted a small room in her lawyer's office and worked like a demon, finally putting the finishing touch to it a fortnight before university began again.

Her marks had been reasonably good: Bs and a few As. This year, she decided, there would be many more As on the lists. She was determined to get as good a degree as she could.

'Do you think you'll like it any more than you did last year?' As expected by everyone but herself, Alex had got straight As, but, sprawled on their lawn in a bikini which barely covered the salient points, she looked more like a pin-up than a brilliant honours student.

Enviously Cathy surveyed her companion's long legs. 'Oh, I think so. Last year I was afraid that I'd fail and everyone would laugh at me for thinking I had a brain. This year I know I can do it. It will take some of the pressure off, and give me a chance to relax and enjoy it. Alex, I don't want to sound carping, but that bikini is indecent!'

Not at all abashed Alex laughed. 'It's one my mother bought me in my last year at school. I think I must have been a little smaller then.'

'You're so lucky. Your legs go right up to your armpits.' Cathy cast herself a disparaging glance. 'Whereas mine seem to stop at my knees.'

'Women who moan about their figures are my pet hate. Anyway, I think you should count your blessings. Everyone treats me as if I were an Amazon, but they act all protective around you. I think I threaten their sense of masculine strength, whereas you reinforce it. Not just men, either. Even women get all motherly with you.'

Cathy gave a snort. 'You must be joking!'

'Only partly.' Alex yawned and rolled over, shielding her face from the sun. 'Cathy, do you want to come to an evening with me?'

'An evening?'

'Well, one of the professors is giving it, so I can hardly call it a party. I'm not all that keen on going but it's a sort of welcome for a guy who's coming to give a course of lectures, and it was made clear that we were expected to be there.'

Cathy forbore to refuse, as was her first impulse. In some ways Alex was endearingly shy, and Cathy couldn't refuse such a simple request.

'OK,' she said cheerfully. 'When is it?'

'A week after the term starts. Thanks, love.'

'No trouble.'

However, Cathy's airy reply was far from her mind when just after she and Alex had walked in through the door she caught a glimpse of a pair of broad shoulders and the proud angle of a dark head.

Of course this had happened before. At first it had been hell to walk down the street; every man over six feet tall had set her heart beating unbearably until she had seen that he was not Jake.

Fiercely telling her senses to stop trying to make a fool of her, she smiled at the host, a shrewd man with a grey beard and pointed eyebrows he was rather proud of, and accepted an offer of a drink, all the time keeping her gaze carefully averted from the man who lounged with Jake's elegant ease against a wall across the room. But like a tongue unable to leave an aching tooth alone, her eyes found their way back. He was standing with his face turned away, his head slightly bent as he talked to someone much shorter than him. As Cathy watched with misery darkening her eyes he suddenly lifted his head and, as though her attention had caught his, he stared straight across to where she stood.

CHAPTER EIGHT

'I HAVE to get out of here,' she hissed at her hapless companion.

Alex had eyes that were large and extremely blue; she turned them on Cathy now, demanding after a bewildered second, 'What on earth are you talking about?'

Cathy was sliding around behind people, her whole will bent on one thing only, getting out of the room before Jake saw her. She said grimly, 'I'll see you back at the flat.'

'But *Cathy*,' Alex wailed, following. 'What's got into you?'

Fascinated, she broke off as a lean form seemed to materialise out of nowhere, interposing itself between Cathy and the door.

'Hello, Cathy,' Jake said calmly. 'Leaving so soon?'

She snapped upright but had to take a deep breath when the world swung around her head. 'Oh, Jake,' she said inanely.

Unholy mockery crackled in his sea-coloured eyes. As always she felt herself weakening, and as always she fought the treachery within. Her gaze fell on Alex, who was standing with her lovely mouth slightly open while her eyes flicked from Jake's angular features to Cathy's carefully composed face.

Offered a prop by convention she introduced them, gratified because she didn't stumble over his name and perversely furious because Alex's beautiful face instantly assumed an expression of pure hero-worship.

'Jake Ferrers,' Alex breathed. 'Oh, goodness, I heard a rumour, but there are so many . . . Are you really coming here to lecture for a term?'

'I believe so,' he drawled, apparently not in the least averse to having the most beautiful, and probably the most brilliant,

132

woman in the room melting in a little pile at his feet.

Cathy felt sick. She had no intention of attracting attention to herself by saying anything and was in the process of retreating behind a large woman dressed in what appeared to be a patchwaork quilt when she felt his hand reach out and clasp hers with a warning pressure.

'I wish you'd stand still,' he complained, smiling sunnily down at her with eyes which were cold and hard and bright. 'You're such a tiny thing, it's difficult to see you at the best of times without this habit you've developed of hiding behind people. How are you?'

Sheer rage held her upright, forced her to meet his aggression with spirited confidence. 'I am very well,' she said sweetly. 'And you?'

'Like you, very well.'

The note of mockery in his voice shredded the last remnant of self-preservation. In tones which dripped with honey she asked, 'And your sister? How is she?'

His hand clenched so tightly around the fragile bones of her wrist that she gasped. Instantly she was released and she had the odd feeling that he hadn't even realised he had done it. His lashes drooped over pinpoints of light as he returned smoothly, 'She's having a difficult time at the moment, but I'm sure that she and her husband will be able to work things out.'

'Again?' Cathy sighed dulcetly. 'Dear me, she does have bad luck, doesn't she. I wondered what had brought you back, but I should have known immediately that it had to be the return of Superbrother.'

Alex gasped, her eyes so wide-stretched that they looked completely round. She took one look at the darkly furious face of the man who stood so threateningly over Cathy and interposed in a hushed voice, 'Are you going to come to blows? Because if you are I think it's only fair that you should have some sort of handicap, Mr Ferrers. I could tie one hand behind your back.'

Oh, bless you, Alex, Cathy thought, already wondering what on earth had made her so stupid as deliberately to provoke that formidable temper. She cast a fleeting glance up at Jake and saw the black fury in his expression begin to fade into controlled wry humour.

'Miss—Alex?' he drawled after a further tense moment. 'It is clear to me that you are every bit as wise as you are beautiful. However, you can't have known Cathy for long. She is more than capable of winning her own battles without any need for handicaps.'

Alerted by an odd note in his voice, Cathy looked up sharply; his lips were twisted in a far from pleasant smile as he finished, 'Your protective instincts do you credit. Restore my faith in femininity, in fact.' He smiled at Alex and then at Cathy and perhaps only she could see that his eyes were like aquamarines, deep and sparkling and entirely without warmth.

Alex swallowed and said tentatively, 'Cath, I have to go and see—er—someone——'

'Cathy will wait here,' Jake said smoothly, giving her a smile of such charm that it was all Alex could do to walk steadily away from them.

Cathy didn't even see her go. Her whole being was focused on the man who stood so easily beside her, looking down at her with a face fierce-hewn in predatory angles. He was all watchful animal, hunting a prey at last within his grasp.

Unease was a sliver of ice down her spine. She said stiffly, 'I don't want to be here.'

'I can see that. Frightened you might learn to want me again, Cathy?'

Trust him, she thought bitterly, remembering the pain and the humiliation, still raw and aching in her. Between her teeth she countered, 'No, that's not an issue. I don't have to have my nose rubbed in my own stupidity. I must be more like my grandfather than I'd thought, because one thing I don't forgive is betrayal.'

'And that's what you think I did to you? Betrayed you? Is all this arrogant scorn because my sister needed me more than you did?'

His words hurt, especially as she had wondered if perhaps she had been too easily hurt by his care for Emma. Then she thought of that wild, ecstatic mating, and his rejection after it, and she brought her head up proudly. Nothing, not even his sense of responsibility, could excuse that. He had used her, and he was clearly not in the least sorry for it.

Stonily, her face politely empty of feeling, she said, 'I can see that we must agree to disagree.'

'If you don't bear me a grudge because I felt that Emma needed me more than you did, then it must be that you regret what happened that last time on the island.'

She couldn't hide the flush his words brought, but she said nothing, folding her lips in a defiant line.

He smiled unpleasantly. 'I gave you the chance to refuse me, Cathy. A chance you didn't take.'

Her lashes lifted; she looked into his tough aggressive face with eyes which were flat and hard like blue pebbles. 'The only reason I'm inclined to accept what you did is that you thought you were helping your sister. I won't bore you with telling you that you are the reason their marriage is in trouble——'

'It is not in trouble.'

'But you said——'

'I said that she is having a difficult time. Which she is. Morning sickness can be extremely debilitating.' He was watching her keenly, his expression shuttered. When she said nothing, her cold proud face remaining unaltered, he went on with sudden anger, 'Do you honestly believe that the reason they had such a problem at the beginning was that Emma was stupid enough to hold me up as an example to Peter? Is that how you justified sleeping with Peter?'

She laughed, a wicked taunting little laugh which should

have warned him. Over the width of his shoulder she could see their host bearing down on them wearing an arch look which meant that they were going to be interrupted.

'Oh, no,' she purred, leaning forward so that her face was close to his chest. He bent his head so that he could hear as she confided in a husky, sensuous whisper, 'I slept with Peter because I am promiscuous and very, very passionate. As I remember you telling me one memorable occasion when that control you're so proud of cracked into a million pieces.'

She stepped into him, pressed her body against his for the second it took him to react, made a sensuous little grind of her hips, and even as his hands shot out to grab her shoulders she was stepping back, malice glinting in her eyes, when he had to turn to greet the man who clapped him on the shoulder.

Cathy turned and fled, cursing herself for following that wild, foolish impulse. When Alex arrived home an hour later she was crouched in her chair, her eyes wild, her hands systematically shredding a handkerchief.

Alex gave her a long, sympathetic look before going into the kitchen to make camomile tea.

'Filthy stuff,' Cathy said automatically, but she began to drink it. About half-way through she asked with abrupt and elaborate unconcern, 'How long is he going to be here?'

'A term.' Alex didn't have to ask who they were talking about.

Cathy grimaced and drank some more tea, her face white and strained. Then she said fiercely, 'Well, I'm not going to run.'

'No.'

'The campus is big enough to hold us both. I'll probably never even see him again. And I'm not in love with him any more.'

'Of course you're not.' Alex's voice was soothing.

Cathy looked across at her and smiled without humour. 'I promise you I'm not. The man's an arrogant, cheating bastard.'

'Sexy, too.'

Cathy laughed. 'Oh, he's that,' she said cynically. 'It doesn't seem fair, does it, for a man to have everything? He looks like every woman's fantasy, he's more than brilliant, and he's got that purely animal magnetism which means that he doesn't need either of the other two qualities.'

'Money, too.' At Cathy's blank stare Alex elaborated. 'Lots of it. His thrillers earn him enormous advances so I suppose the royalties are equally huge.'

'It's just as well that he's also a card-carrying swine.'

Alex's gurgle of laughter brought a wan smile to Cathy's face. She sighed and said wearily, 'Thank you for not asking me questions, Alex.'

'My pleasure. Any time you feel like venting a little more spleen let me know. And now I think it would be a good idea if we went to bed. I have an essay to finish tomorrow, and didn't I hear you muttering about work you wanted to do?'

Alex was right. But as she lay sleeplessly in her bed Cathy discovered that she would have been better off doing something that took her mind off Jake. At first she ran through a list of adjectives she had subconsciously been collecting over the last year; that was satisfying, but eventually it failed to keep her mind off the fact that behind her eyelids she could see him so clearly, as though he were in the room with her. He had looked—tired, his splendid vitality faded. The creases at the corners of his eyes were a little deeper, his beautiful mouth set in slightly more cynical lines.

It seemed that the last year hadn't been one of unalloyed satisfaction for him. She was horrified to find herself wondering anxiously what had happened to dim his vitality, and had to tell herself very firmly that whatever it was was no concern of hers. She hoped he had suffered twice the pain he had caused her.

As she finally dropped off to sleep she was muttering that

she did not love him, never had loved him. It was only infatuation.

Which was true, but did not explain why she woke in the morning with a headache and the dry, hot eyes of someone who has been weeping in her sleep. And when at last, after a long time spent in the bathroom removing the traces of tears, she went into the kitchen, Alex sent her a sympathetic glance before pushing the coffee-pot towards her.

More than anything in the world Cathy wanted to stay silent, but she had to ask gruffly, 'Did I wake you up last night?'

'Oh—once or twice. Bad dreams are hell, aren't they.'

Cathy drank some coffee and said on a rush, 'I think the day you decided to live here was a very lucky one for me.'

Alex gave her beautiful smile. 'For me too. Now, what do we need in the grocery line today? It's my week to shop.'

And all was back to normal.

Only it wasn't. Cathy had to force herself to go into university and once she was there she developed an uneasy, hunted feeling between her shoulder-blades.

What made the whole thing totally ridiculous was that she never set eyes on Jake. Because of the man he was she heard a lot about him; however, as she had said, the campus was a big place, and she certainly never saw him. But still she felt a certain kind of doomed sensation, and it began to put her off her work. Then one day she was handed back a paper with some extremely caustic comments on the bottom and she realised that once again she was allowing Jake Ferrers to screw up her life.

So she put him very firmly to the back of her mind and settled down to some hard work.

Until one day as she was running for a bus she heard her name and stopped, turning a red, exasperated face towards the man who had stopped at the kerb and was stretching over to open the door for her.

'Pete!' she said, and her lovely smile lit up her face.

He shouted, 'For God's sake get in, the lights are going to change,' and before she had time to reconsider she was in the front seat.

Sure enough the lights flashed green and he set the car in motion, saying with a trace of hesitation, 'How are you?'

'Fine. And you?'

'Not too bad,' he said more easily.

'And Emma?'

A longer pause and he said, 'Well, she's pretty good too. After that—a year or so ago she was pretty miserable, but she tried hard and she snapped out of it. She says she grew up. Actually, we're still seeing a marriage guidance counsellor.'

'That's good,' she said a little awkwardly.

He muttered something at a driver who cut too closely around the corner and said, 'Where are you heading? I'll drop you off.'

And when she had given her address he said, 'I thought—I wanted to tell you that I'm sorry I told Emma about you and Addison. It was a lousy thing to do.'

'It's all right,' she said, feeling obscurely sorry for him.

He slanted a wary smile at her. 'No, it's not all right. I don't even know why I did. It certainly never occurred to me that she'd not only tell Jake but set him on to you.'

'She must have been desperate,' Cathy pointed out drily. 'Understandable, if she thought that we were having an affair.'

Pete's fair skin took on a ruddy hue. 'I did tell her she was a fool for thinking that,' he said belligerently, 'but—oh, hell, I suppose I was quite pleased that it hurt her. She'd made a pretty good job of shattering my confidence with her continual comparisons with Jake. I suppose I thought that what was sauce for the goose . . . But honestly, Cath, although I still feel sick when I think of what she tried to do, the lies she told, I can't be sorry, because she knew then that she had gone too far. It took that totally over-the-top scheme of hers to make her admit that she needed help.'

Cathy tried to look sympathetic while thinking that she should be glad that someone had gained from the sordid incident. For the life of her she couldn't think of anything to say.

After a few stretched moments Peter went on, 'And in a way it brought me to my senses. I suppose I was a little possessive where you were concerned. When I saw you with Jake I felt—well, it doesn't matter, but it opened my eyes to realising that perhaps Emma did have cause for complaint with my attitudes. I tried to contact you but I couldn't. Bloody Addison wouldn't tell me where you were. He was damned nasty about it, too,' he finished in an aggrieved tone.

'It's all right,' she said again.

He continued awkwardly but with determination, as though he had to purge himself of something, 'Things got a bit confused after that. We had a rough time for a few weeks. She was determined to divorce me but Jake talked her out of that. Then she sort of collapsed. I think it was a nervous breakdown of sorts, and that's when I realised that she really did need me. More to the point, she realised it herself. Jake wouldn't do. He was in filthy mood for weeks, impatient and angry. Actually, he was bloody unpleasant to both of us.' He grimaced. 'Emma got no sympathy from him, so she had to fall back on me. She's changed, Cathy.'

Cathy listened, wondering just how right he was. Aloud she said, 'I was talking to Jake the other day. He said she's pregnant. How does she feel about that?'

He grinned, all complacent male. 'She's pleased as Punch, although she's having a bad bout with morning sickness, poor kid.'

'Well, that's good.' Cathy's voice was falsely hearty. She moved her shoulders uneasily as she sensed his sideways appraisal.

Too much had happened for them to feel anything like the

old camaraderie, but there was more than a hint of it in his words when he said, 'I told Jake that we hadn't had an affair, Cath, but he didn't believe me. Do you want me to convince him?'

'I don't,' she bit out, 'care twopence about Jake Ferrers, and I couldn't care less about what he thinks of me.'

'Oh.' He frowned. 'Then what we saw——?'

Cathy sighed. 'He's an attractive man,' she said reluctantly. 'I'm not immune.'

'Do you still think that he knew of Emma's plan to burst in on you?'

More than anything she wanted to forget the whole business, but perhaps she owed Peter this. 'No,' she said. 'No. He's not the sort. In his own way Jake is an honourable man.'

'I'm sorry it didn't work out for you.' He hesitated, before adding, 'He stormed around like a caged tiger when he got back from the island. Emma said she'd never known him to be so sarcastic and angry. He was sheer hell to live with.'

'I imagine that's par for the course,' she said between clenched teeth. 'Frustration is not——' She stopped precipitately, furious with herself.

Suddenly highly amused, Peter gave an unrepentant grin. 'You're probably right. Well, I'm not going to interfere.'

Cathy turned a diamond bright gaze on him. Very precisely, she said, 'There is nothing for you to interfere in.'

'Of course there's not,' he said soothingly, chuckling in an odious fashion as he drew in to the kerb. 'You are just good enemies. I'll see you to the door.'

'You will not,' she said crisply. 'It's still broad daylight.'

She opened the door and was out before he could unclip his seat-belt. Stooping down, she said firmly through the window, 'Thank you for the ride home, Pete. I'm glad you're happy now.'

'So am I,' he said, and got out to come around the front. He was smiling, but she could see the hint of pleading beneath the lightweight charm, and braced herself. Tentatively he touched her cheek and said, 'I really am sorry, Cathy. I was unfair on you, and with very little excuse. I got to thinking, you see, that I'd be a lot happier if I'd chosen you. I didn't stop to think. Forgive me?'

She nodded, and reached up to kiss him on the cheek. It was an end, and they could go no further. Peter had come to realise that his first loyalty must always be to his wife, and Cathy had learned to put away the childish hungering for acceptance which had made his affection so important.

Now, smiling mistily, she waved him goodbye before turning up the walk to the house. And there, striding down the path, came Jake, his hard face set in a mask of anger.

And happiness burst into glorious freedom, running wild through Cathy's body in a stunning, freewheeling response, singing in every nerve-end, so that she knew that down all the years, through the long days of her life, she would remember this moment and her eager, laughing acceptance of it, because whatever happened she was in love with him, and she would cherish it like a lovely secret for eternity.

But at the moment her love was in a black fury and she knew why. Before he had a chance to speak she held up her hand in an authoritative, sharp gesture.

'That,' she said deliberately, 'was the first time I've seen him for over a year, and we were saying goodbye; we won't be seeing each other again except in the normal course of socialising. So you have no need to come over all protective for your sister.'

He had stopped a few feet away and was watching her as though she was something insignificant, something he could crush easily in those strong hands.

But when he spoke his voice was surprisingly mild. 'I see. Just an accidental meeting.'

She knew that tone. A little pale, she looked up at through the tips of her lashes. 'Yes.'

In a voice as smooth and fierce as molten metal he said, 'See that it's the last.'

Her shoulders stiffened. 'You have no right to demand that. I give you my word that there is nothing between Pete and me now. If you must know, he was apologising for using me.'

'How—tactful of him,' he snarled, strange dark patches of colour highlighting the arrogant cheekbones. 'And I suppose you have forgiven him! You don't set a very high value on your favours, do you? Or yourself.'

She opened her mouth to fire back an answer, saw the anticipatory glitter beneath his lashes and closed it very firmly. So he had come here to pick a fight, had he? She was no longer a whipping-boy for him; he could go to hell!

Infusing her voice with maddening reason, she said sweetly, 'I hadn't actually thought of it that way, but you could be right. Now, what can I do for you?'

'Nothing.' He had whipped his temper back under control, using that cold determination she feared. His mouth curled in a slow, unpleasant smile. 'I actually came to see your flatmate, Alex Severn. She may not have told you, but she's in one of my tutorials. A brilliant woman. She should go far.'

'Beautiful, too,' she agreed cordially. 'But, best of all, she is utterly, totally dependable and honest and kind.' She flashed him a smile and was glad to see that she had struck home. The predatory glint darkened into something more enigmatic. He hesitated, then stood aside as she started off up the path.

Over her shoulder she said airily, 'She won't be home until seven o'clock, but if you want to wait that's all right.'

'Kind of you.' The words were rapped out but almost absently, as though he was thinking of something else.

'Oh, not at all. I know you won't steal anything.' The lock clicked. She pushed the door open and walked into the hall. 'I have to leave in half an hour, but I'm sure you'll be able to find yourself something to do while you wait.'

'Where are you going?'

'Out.'

Both question and answer were delivered in a peremptory voice, both opponents then looking a little startled as though the words had come unbidden. They stood in the shadowy, slightly stuffy hall, the tall dark man poised with the lean arrogance of perfect healthy, perfect confidence, and the small woman, her beautiful face withdrawn yet composed, staring at each other like long-time enemies, neither prepared to give quarter.

And emotion drummed between them, unspoken but powerful, the strength of it producing exactly the same taut reserve in each face.

He said slowly, 'You look—older.'

You look exhausted.

Outside on the cool reaches of the lawn a blackbird called its alarm cry. Cathy felt its urgency, the primal warning to flee, and had to brace herself not to obey it.

Suddenly, as if the words were dragged from him, he said, 'I was afraid that Emma would have a breakdown as she did when our parents were killed. She tried to commit suicide. It took years and a variety of therapies before we managed to get her life into some sort of order. I could see the whole thing happening again, if someone didn't prevent it. She's not very stable, even now. I'd been responsible for her for so long—and Peter seems a damned weak prop to keep her upright. I felt that my first obligation was to her.'

'I know.'

In exactly the same tone he said, 'You are a tough little thing, sophisticated and sharp and spoilt. But occasionally I got the impression that you were playing a game . . . that beneath that glossy surface there was a different, vulnerable Cathy. I wondered.'

She looked at him consideringly. She loved him. How easy to say, how strangely simple. She could tell him, let him see how he had hurt her, get a little revenge. But if she did that he would apologise, and go away and she would never see him again. She knew that as clearly as if he had told her. Whenever he thought of her he would always feel a little guilty; he had standards, and he valued innocence. Like all truly strong men, he was innately protective.

And she wanted to see him. Oh, she was probably putting herself in the firing line for more pain, because what would a man like Jake, brilliant, sophisticated, courted, have in common with Cathy Durrant, who was not finding it all that easy to get an economics degree? Apart, of course, from this damned inconvenient passion which threatened to send them both up in flames every time they saw each other.

But she had to try.

So she said coolly, 'You hurt my pride. I was angry because you accepted that I'd had an affair with Peter just because Emma said so.'

'And that was untrue? Peter didn't make any attempt to deny it until afterwards.'

Her lips twisted. With a cutting irony she said, 'Emma had managed to strip him of self-confidence. Do you know, she used to rail at him if he didn't attract a waiter's eye fast enough and tell him that you always intimidated even head waiters. I think he was grateful for anything, even a lie, which made him feel a man.'

She couldn't see what he was thinking. The chiselled contours of his face were dark against the shadowed wall. He looked down at her as though his mind was far away.

Then he said slowly, 'Is that the truth?'

'I don't lie.' *Except by omission.*

'You didn't go to bed with Peter?'

She looked at him steadily. 'No.'

She flinched when he put out a hand to lift her chin. His fingers were warm and strong and merciless; he held her face tilted up towards him while eyes like splintered ice searched her face. Then he said with a derisive mocking note, 'Ah, what the hell . . . Women lie and don't even think to count the cost.'

But as she closed her eyes to hide from the pitiless cynicism he bent his head and his mouth touched the little pulse throbbing like a bird's song in its throat, and the singing in her blood became transmuted into thunder, overwhelming, shattering the remnants of control, obliterating her disappointment and his contempt in a cataclysm of sensuality.

It was not enough. It had not been enough the first time he kissed her. Desire was no toy, no easily manipulated object; it was an elemental force, the blind urge to perpetuate the species cunningly intertwined with such exquisite sensations that it was almost impossible to resist. Cathy made no attempt; she swayed towards the lean tightly held strength of his body and said something inarticulate, her voice husky and impeded.

He laughed, a short, mirthless sound, and said against her skin, 'I could lay you down here and you'd let me, wouldn't you.'

His voice made her shiver with wild longings but it broke the spell. Slowly she fought back the storm, until at last she dared look at him.

He was watching her with merciless intentness. The blue-green shards of diamond in his eyes were the only sign of colour; tanned skin was stretched tight over the hard contours of his face. He looked as arrogantly confident as an eagle.

'No,' she said, pulling away carefully, as though an unwise movement could call back that firestorm of sensation.

His eyes flashed to the painful little messenger in her throat. Almost absently he said, 'You are so small . . . I feel as though I could break you, and yet you're as tough as tempered steel.'

'Hardly,' she returned grimly, desperate to sever that eye-contact, to free herself from the casual unbreakable grip of his hands. 'I'm flesh and blood. When I'm hurt I bleed and bruise, just like everyone else.'

His face hardened. 'But you make sure you leave your mark,' he said, and she flinched, because it sounded like the smoothest of threats, grounded in emotions too deep and strong to be denied.

The muscles in the smooth length of her throat moved. 'What exactly does that mean?'

'Oh, that you have left me with a few unfulfilled fantasies.' He smiled and his eyes correctly read the import of her dilating pupils. 'Yes. Fantasies of taking you, of stamping myself on you so strongly that whenever you go to bed with another man it will be my face you see at your breasts, my hands you feel on your body, I who possess you and wring the last ounce of enjoyment from the hot, sweet sheath of you. Primitive fantasies, chauvinist and despicable, and so potent that for a year now they've coloured my dreams in all the erotic hues of passion.'

His hand left a trail of fire across her throat; the lean fingers found the trembling curves of her mouth and slid in through her lips, somehow making them his. Cathy felt the tang of his masculinity on her tongue, and tried to pull away but he held her with a casual ease which was insulting, pulling his hand away to lift his fingers to his mouth.

It was an oddly passionate little gesture; Cathy took a painful breath and let it out in a long noiseless sigh.

'Warm,' he said, his expression absorbed and intent. 'Sweet as honey, and as fierce as fire. I think it's time I indulged a few of those fantasies, Cathy. You've left me with a hunger in my blood which only you can appease. I want you. And I'm going to have you.'

The threat rang stark and terrifying in the quiet hall. Cathy turned her face away because his determination blazed forth with such power that she felt it in the deepest marrow of her bones. And unwillingly, but oh, so strongly, the tides of life and nature began to push through her body in their slow inexorable way, stealthy and remorseless, summoning up all the old atavistic hungers, purely female, primal as the first intimations of sexuality.

It took all her resolution to step away from him but she did it, because although her body was surrendering to his potent warfare her eyes told her that all she could see in his face, her ears warned her that all that was in his voice was lust.

And her heart knew that while she loved him he felt nothing so glorious, nothing so painful for her.

Quite distinctly, she said, 'You've already had me. Remember?'

'It wasn't,' he said through lips that barely moved, 'enough. I remember. You were so tiny you should have been totally at my mercy, but in the end it was I who was taken and used.'

She lifted her head proudly and before he could speak continued pointedly, 'Are you so conceited that you think I should be honoured by the fact that you want me? You, the great genius, honouring an ordinary woman with your lust?'

Instead of the anger she was prepared for he reacted with a wry, bleak smile. 'Ordinary? Is that how you see yourself? Oh no, Cathy, no *ordinary* woman could cause as much havoc as you have in your short life. An ordinary woman wouldn't have blackmailed Trent Addison into marriage—or kept both him and his wife as friends afterwards. Ordinary women don't have this ability to burn themselves into a man's brain and body, until he becomes less of a man for his hunger. Do you think I go around telling ordinary women that I want them, have to have them? I do not. You have power, Cathy, and I've become ensnared in your spell, but I want out. And I don't really care how I get out.'

Appalled at the open self-contempt in his voice, she stared at him, her skin white and oddly cold, her eyes so wide that the irises were almost engulfed by the blackness of the pupils. Yet she was excited, and fiercely pleased, because there had been torment running deep in the remorseless current of his words, buried like jagged rocks in a stream, and for the first time perhaps he had been open and honest with her.

Instinct told her that this was painful and rare with him.

Into her mind came an image of the little boy who had been sent away to boarding-school at the age of four. Had he decided then that he was never going to love, because it was too painful?

She said suddenly, 'When you were sent to school, how did you cope?'

And without thought he said, 'Oh, they let me keep my teddy bear, but they didn't approve of tears. Geniuses don't cry. They're above such mortal weaknesses.'

'Poor little boy,' she said quietly.

He showed his teeth. 'I enjoyed myself there, and I certainly got a far better education than would have been possible in an ordinary school, so don't go feeling sorry for me.'

'I thought you had me tagged as a woman who was incapable of any finer feelings.'

He laughed, saying with cruel carelessness, 'No, not at all. You make love like a divine witch.'

'All that that proves,' she returned deliberately, 'is that, like many men, you confuse sensation with emotion, and lust with desire. Go away, Jake. Find some other IQ groupie to satisfy those inconvenient needs of yours. I have better things to do with my time.'

CHAPTER NINE

HER choice of words was specific and deliberate. He had spoken as though she were just a body for which he had developed an inconvenient passion; to revenge herself for the insult she implied that his wonderful creative brain was only thing that mattered of Jake Ferrers. She had depersonalised him as he had done her.

She lifted her chin, daring him to react with the violence she sensed so close to the surface. But with incredible will, so integral a part of the enigma that was Jake, he controlled that first impulse to maim and punish.

The long hands deliberately relaxed. In an arrested voice he said, 'Very clever, Cathy. You're a worth-while antagonist. Just remember, I don't admit defeat. Ever.'

Reaching out, he hooked a finger through the brilliant tangle of her hair, smoothing the lock back from her forehead. An ironic smile curled the beautiful contours of his mouth, softening the hard line into something closely approaching amusement and complicity. He bent his head to touch his mouth to the white temple he had exposed and whispered, 'Not in my work, not in my life. This, my small angel of darkness, is a duel to the finish. And I have no compunction about the choice of weapons. When you sob again with that small death in my arms I'll remind you of this moment.'

As a parting shot it was hard to better. Cathy's hand crept up to her heart, clenched protectively over it while she watched his lean-hipped stride through the door and down the path.

But lightening the panic and the ice-cold conviction that

this time he was after the subjugation of her soul, there flashed a laughing, reckless defiance. Generations of pirates in her ancestry lifted their heads and watched with her, their eyes flashing with anticipation. So, he thought it was going to be a simple task to get her into his bed, purge himself of this wretched ache in his body, did he? And then send her on her way while he went back to his enjoyable buccaneering around the world!

She laughed. Peter could have warned him that in the days of their childhood people had been known to turn pale at that wicked chuckle. But Peter wasn't there, and there was no one else to hear, no one to warn the man who had strode so arrogantly through the door.

When Alex arrived home Cathy was sitting at the table in the kitchen, drinking coffee and writing a letter. Looking up, she smiled with such radiance that Alex blinked.

'Good news?' she asked.

Cathy grinned mysteriously. 'Depends what you call good news.'

'Jake Ferrers has been here.'

Cathy looked alarmed. 'Is it that obvious?'

'To me it is. Ever since I've known you you've looked—oh, muted, I suppose is as good a word as any. And then you met him at that wretched party and you blazed into life. You've got that same look now. As if you'd been walking around in a cloak of shadows, and someone has ripped it away.'

'Mathematicians,' Cathy told her loftily, 'are not supposed to go in for flights of fancy. Even mathematicians who indulge in English Lit. on the side.'

But secretly she couldn't help but admit that Alex had said it exactly. The last year—no, all her life—had been a prelude to this moment. The fact that she loved Jake had transformed her. It almost didn't matter that he didn't love her, probably never would. When he walked out of her life he would leave behind a raw wound which might not heal, but she could not regret this glorious experience of loving.

She had never been able to understand how people could die for love, sacrifice all for what seemed to her to be such an ephemeral emotion. Her one experience of it, her infatuation for Trent, had left her disillusioned and sad.

This, oh, *this* was different. This was everything the poets had written and more. This, she thought exultantly, was worth fighting for. This emotion was its own reward.

But what did she know of tactics? The only thing she could remember of value was an injunction to carry the war into the enemy's camp. Which was not a lot of help.

Her frown lifted slightly as she decided that merely knowing that she loved Jake gave her an edge, a pivot of knowledge she could exploit to get him off balance. He would come looking for her—and when he did, she would be more than ready for him!

Alex had been watching her with some anxiety. This Cathy was a woman she did not know, her extraordinary beauty enhanced greatly by a sort of incandescence—and, she realised with a sinking heart, a blazing recklessness which added a stunning sparkle of challenge to the delicate features.

'I don't know,' she said diffidently, 'that I'd like to take Jake Ferrers on. At anything.'

Cathy grinned. 'Frightens you, does he?'

'Don't try to tell me he doesn't scare the hell out of you!'

'All right, I won't, but I'm not afraid of him, because he's already done the worst thing he possibly can to me.'

Alex looked appalled. 'Then—no, I won't pry.'

'You wouldn't know how to,' Cathy told her affectionately. 'And no, he didn't rape me. But the thing is, Jake thinks he knows me really well. And he doesn't, not at all. Whereas I know I don't know anything about him, so I won't be over-confident.'

'Oh, you have a way with words,' Alex said gloomily. 'That's as clear as mud. I only hope you do know what you're doing. Jake Ferrers is dangerous.'

'So,' Cathy said, narrowing her eyes and smiling in an explicitly sinister way, 'am I.'

Alex laughed but went away shaking her head, leaving Cathy to finish her letter, then sit for long minutes staring dreamily into space. Jake could behave like a swine; it was time he learned that he couldn't go about breaking hearts with such cynical abandon. Even Cathy might have been frightened by his reputation if she hadn't known that he was not all steel; he loved and was very protective of his sister. And then . . .

From the vantage point of a year Cathy found herself remembering how good a companion he had been on the island, how interesting and fascinating she had found him. For the whole of the last year she had pretended that it was his blatant masculinity which had attracted her, because that was the only way she could deal with the pain. Hurt pride she could manage; a love that might last a lifetime was too frightening.

But she had not been duped by a charmingly charismatic cheat. The moment she saw him again she had realised that hurt pride was the least of her worries. She loved the man who had revealed himself to her, however unwillingly, on the island, who had struck sparks off her brain, who had excited her and irritated her and made her think harder than she had ever done before. He was not a tender man, but he had shown her moments of great tenderness. She had sought him in Trent but he was already in love with another; she should have waited for Jake instead of rashly setting out to bag her man. But that mistake had given her experience; using it, she knew she had picked the right man this time.

All she had to do now was convince him.

He let a week go by before he made any move, and even then it could merely have been a coincidence which brought him to the Domain on a fine windy Saturday to watch the kites flying.

But Cathy didn't think so. That secret instinct had warned her of his approach some moments before he finally came to a stop beside her so she was able to turn her face up with a smile as wide and innocent as any child's, the bright depths of her eyes sparkling with pleasure.

'Another frustrated kite-flyer?' she asked demurely.

He looked very big, very handsome beside her; she had already noticed the stir of interest among the women around them. Now he smiled, and an odd sensation shivered up her backbone.

'Is that why you're here? Because you never had a kite to fly in your youth? Poor little rich girl.'

She reacted to the mockery in the deep voice with laughter. It was, she thought fleetingly, just as well that she had decided on her tactics; she could enjoy the battle so much more.

'Alas, no. Pete and I had hundreds, I was forever losing mine. I suppose I enjoy them because I have so many happy memories. His father used to bring us here often.'

He definitely didn't like it when she brought Peter into the conversation. The sea-coloured eyes hardened but after a tingling moment he said calmly, 'So you do have some happy memories.'

'Lots. Children have a great capacity for making the best of things, as you should know. I had a happy childhood.'

'Who wouldn't, spoiled and cosseted and indulged, your every desire satisfied?'

'Is it possible to have every desire satisfied?' Her face was grave, her voice deliberately sombre. 'I used to want my father.'

He sent her a sharp, altogether too perceptive glance, and smiled, not at all pleasantly, although when he spoke his voice was deceptively mild. 'Pitching it a bit strong, Cathy. If you want me to feel sorry for you you'll have to do better than that.'

She laughed, flinging her head back in real enjoyment, and this time she did surprise him. It gave her immense satisfaction to see the wariness in his face, hastily obliterated though it was, satisfaction and a kind of bitter pleasure. She would have liked to be able to look at him with her love plain for everyone to see, to have him gaze back at her in the same way, but as she couldn't do that she would take pleasure where she could.

'Don't you think I have any of the usual emotions?' she asked provocatively.

But this was a mistake. Boredom replaced the all too elusive interest in his expression. 'I believe that you missed your father a little,' he said aloofly, 'but I know that you saw little of him. He and your mother lived a very social life. So you must excuse me for doubting that you spent your childhood yearning for him. As for the other . . .' that unpleasant smile curled his mouth below eyes that were scornful as he bent his head until it was only a breath away from hers '. . . of course I believe you feel all the usual emotions. Perhaps more than is good—or wise. And the same goes for a few less civilised ones, like revenge. I know you, Cathy.'

She laughed. Swift as a snake she stretched up, still laughing, and kissed his cold, beautiful mouth, her own warm and vulnerable for a moment until she snatched it away.

But if she had hoped he would reciprocate she had forgotten that immense will. She saw the sparks in his eyes and for a moment her hopes rode high until he said softly and icily, 'I don't go in for spectator sports. When I kiss you it will be properly, in private, with a bed handy so that I can do what I want to you.'

The words made her stomach clench; she covered it with a toss of her head, saying airily, 'That's the problem with the modern man! So serious, turning the whole thing into work! What harm can a kiss do?'

'Do you like hearing me admit that I find it difficult to control myself with you?' He looked at her as if he hated her. 'Does it feed your ego, Cathy?'

Her quick, unwanted fear must have shown because he continued in a flat, threatening monotone, 'Enjoy it while you can. You damned near ruined my sister's life with your belief that fundamentally sex is only a pleasant way of passing the time. I'm going to teach you that it's no frivolous plaything. By the time I've finished with you you'll know it for the potent force it is.'

She looked at him seriously. 'And you? You're going to use this potent force to punish? Isn't that doing what you've just accused me of doing, trivialising it? Or do the rules for women not apply to men?'

Dark colour showed against the high contours of his cheekbones. He said between his teeth, 'I don't know. All I know is that you have to be shown that you can't go around sleeping with whoever you want to.'

'Because it makes you jealous.'

'Damn you! Very well then, because it makes me jealous!' He flung the words at her as if they were spears, barbed and deadly, unerringly aimed at the most vulnerable part of her, her heart. 'Last time I drew back because I had some weird idea of honour, but it was wasted because honour means nothing to you, it goes down the drain when it's a question of your own desires. You're avid for sex yet you're used to being the one who makes the rules. Well, not this time, Cathy. Pushing me as hard and as fast as you can is not going to make me lose my head. I can control myself, and I'll decide when I'm ready. I want you starving for it, completely off balance, so hungry that you know at last just how they feel, those men you've tormented and tantalised with your beautiful witch's face and all the lying promise of your sultry little body. For once in your life, Cathy, you're going to know what it's like to want something and be unable to get your greedy little fingers on it. You'll find out what it's like to die of wanting, to need someone so badly that the wanting is like sweet poison in your throat. Then, when you're ready to beg, that's when I'll be ready, and nothing is going to stop me from taking you! Nothing.'

Something didn't ring true. Oh, there was deadly purpose in his tone, and his features were set in an expression of cold anticipation which made her shiver, but she felt—disorientated, almost bewildered because beneath the cold passion, like a counter-current in a polar sea, had been a jagged note of desperation!

Then a small boy came toddling along the grass, chasing a shaggy alsatian dog with the total absorption of the very young; just in front of them he tripped and fell, his mouth rounding into a wail of shock. The dog stopped and Cathy fell to her knees, picking the baby up with a practised scoop, smiling into the puckered little face.

His sorrow forgotten, the child reached out a hand and grabbed a lock of hair. Cathy laughed and stood up, cuddling the warm little body against her as she strove to disentangle the clutching fingers while she talked soothingly to him.

Alerted by the dog, an older child in her early teens came shyly up. 'No!' she said sharply to the baby, who reacted by whimpering and clinging even more tightly to the strands of copper in his fat little fist.

'Jason, let go!' His sister grabbed his hand and tried to prise it loose, in the process hurting Cathy more than the baby had.

'Wait, let's see if I can persuade him to do it gently,' she said quickly. 'Come on Jason, unhand me, there's a good boy.' Half crooning, half laughing, she coaxed the chubby fingers loose; the baby crowed with delight and waved a hand around, then, when she was at last free, lifted up his round face.

Shyly his sister said, 'He wants to give you a kiss. He dribbles a bit . . .'

'Kisses,' Cathy said firmly, 'are worth a little bit of dribble.'

She received a wet salute on her chin before reluctantly handing Jason back to his beaming sister who staggered off down the hill with the dog in close attendance.

Cathy waited until they were gone, her face unconsciously wistful, before she groped in her pocket.

'Here,' Jake said curtly. A lean hand tipped her chin so that he could wipe the evidence of Jason's affection from her skin with a large white handkerchief.

She suffered his ministrations with a smooth, immobile face, annoyed because he had caught her at a disadvantage. She was not ready to reveal any of her true self to him, and she had a feeling that he might have read a little too much into the incident. However, a peek from below her lashes reassured her; his face was without expression except for the compressed line of his lips.

'Even babies,' he said calmly, 'fall beneath that spell. Lucky Catherine.'

Her mouth quirked. Quite deliberately she retorted, 'Oh, I don't know. According to Emma you've had to swat women off like flies ever since you realised there were two sexes. I think I'm entitled to a quick conquest or two. I have a very poor track record, when you think of it. A divorce, a friend who thinks nothing of betraying my most intimate secrets, and a lover who only wants me because he can't rid himself of an awkward passion any other way. Jason is rather a salve to my pride.'

'How are the mighty fallen.' But he seemed amused rather than disgusted, and an amused Jake was an altogether different proposition!

Rashly Cathy warmed to the gleam of humour which warmed the sea-coloured eyes; her mouth curved and she chuckled, unaware that her laughter gave her small face an extra vividness, a bright gaiety far removed from her usual sultriness.

His gaze sharpened. For a long second his eyes rested on

the rich curve of her mouth and her heartbeats quickened, pounding high in her throat. Then the enigmatic shutters he could summon at will screened his unwilling appreciation and she was shocked at the disappointment which clutched at her.

But all he said was, 'Very well, then, you can conquer a baby or two, provided there's no one any older panting around you.'

Her brow lifted. Very drily she returned, 'I'm not making any promises.'

He laughed. 'Then, my dear, you'll be responsible for anything that happens to him. I don't like competition, especially when it come to the favours of a woman.'

'What a sweetly old-fashioned turn of phrase you have,' she marvelled, hiding her instinctive fear with sarcasm. The threat had been naked and pointed, a blunt instrument of power directed straight at her throat. 'Tell me, Jake, if there's ever been any competition what have you done in the past?'

He showed his teeth in a smile. 'Got rid of it.'

Just like that. Cathy shook her head, hiding the instinctive *frisson* his words produced. 'Uncivilised,' she said mournfully.

'Yes.'

The single word was delivered in a monotone, flat and crisp and dark with ancient meaning. Cathy's eyes flew up, enormous, dilated in shock. He didn't look uncivilised; far from it, in fact; he was all lean, poised elegance, his clothes complementing the sophisticated aura that surrounded him wherever he went. Yet there were clues; he walked with a lithe predator's gait, alert and dangerous. And the dark face was hewn in no smoothly civilised lines; danger lurked in the arrogantly clear-cut features, stamped the angles and planes of his face.

But it was the eyes which gave the game away. They were

cool and watchful and hard, and beneath the surface beauty of colour there smouldered a primeval male, dominating and uncompromising, supporting the disciplined modern man with a proud formidable authority.

Cathy's mouth quirked into a challenge. 'Consider myself warned?' she said, far from flippantly.

'If you think it's necessary.'

She said quietly, 'Here's a warning for you, Jake. One of these days you're going to find that the simple rules you've lived your life by are not enough any longer. And when you do, I hope to be around to welcome you into membership of the fallible human race.'

A smile twisted the severe line of his mouth. He said coolly, 'Oh, I doubt it, my dear. Unless you reveal hidden talents beyond those you display so obviously for the world to ogle at.'

Cathy's eyes fell, involuntarily sliding down her body to reassure herself that in a fit of absent-mindedness that morning she hadn't dressed herself in a manner more befitting a seductress. No, she wore an old pair of jeans, snugly fitting but not tight, and a large dark blue jersey with a white silk shirt under it. A blue and white and green scarf completed the outfit. Not one that could be considered sexy or obvious, not even to the most susceptible of men, surely.

She lifted her eyes, and in a voice composed entirely of ice crystals said, 'I'm not going to dignify a dig like that with an answer.'

He looked sardonic and a little weary. 'I find it difficult to believe that you don't know that you could be swathed from head to toe in sackcloth and still blaze with sexuality.'

'Don't be stupid!'

Self-consciously she turned away, feeling as though he had branded her for everyone to see with his cynical assessment of her character. Something savage coloured his laughter, yet she had the strangest belief that he was really laughing at himself.

'It's true, but I'm not going to pander any further to your ego by pointing out that most of the men around here have been dividing their attention between the kites and you, with you having a distinct edge. I'll bet that not one of them has failed to wonder whether you deliver all that you promise. And whether I know the answer.'

Heat crawled along her cheekbones. In a voice soft yet distinct she countered, 'And their women are eyeing you up and down, wondering how good you are in bed. We make a good pair, you and I. Sex objects.'

She turned on her heels, angry with him, furious with herself because she could remember just what he was like in bed, the potency and strength of his body and her own mind-blowing response, and she wanted him now, her body was hot with it, she could almost feel the taste of desire on her tongue. Just for a moment she remembered his threats of a few minutes ago and for one really frightening instant her heart quailed. But pride came to her rescue; her straight back stiffened into tempered steel as she walked up the grassy slope.

Although she half expected him to catch her up he let her go, no doubt confident that he had her captured, that he had only to whistle for her to return to his hand like an obedient puppy. Arrogant bloody man, she seethed, conveniently forgetting that she had spent quite a few hours lately brooding on ways and means to do exactly the same to him.

She refused to allow herself to wonder how he planned to put his threats into action, but found out that very day. Actually it was evening, and both he and she were at a play put on in the university's own theatre, Cathy by herself, he with an extremely elegant woman who was making no secret of the fact that she found her escort utterly fascinating.

Appalled at the surge of ungovernable emotion which drowned her rational faculties, Cathy looked away, striving hard for some kind of control over the primitive urge to kill; to her horror she saw her hands form claws in her lap.

The first act of the play made no impression on her at all. The actors could have been mutes for all she heard; they gestured and moved, the trained voices extracting the last ounce of meaning from each word, each cadence, and all that impinged on Cathy was Jake's dark head silhouetted against the darkness behind, the sharply sculptured profile outlined in cruel symmetry as he kept his eyes on the stage.

That he knew she was there was impossible, yet when the curtain came down to a wave of somewhat startled applause, and the lights came up, he turned his arrogant head and looked straight at her, his mouth compressed.

Cathy's breath hurt in her lungs. A red haze clouded her mind; it took all her considerable will-power not to go across and slap him senseless, because he had deliberately done this, he had wanted her to know what it was like to see him with another woman.

After a moment the woman with him said something and he turned away and got to his feet, helping her up with a hand at her elbow. She slipped and his hand tightened, moved swiftly to her waist. She said something and laughed, and he laughed too, charming her so that she gazed adoringly up into his face, her expression only too easy to read.

Cathy's teeth ground together but she sat still, refusing to give him the satisfaction of knowing how wounded she was.

She was half afraid that he would seek her out but he didn't, and after what had been the worst evening in her whole life she managed to slip away through the crush of people without setting eyes on either of her tormentors again.

At home she made herself a pot of herb tea and sat drinking it, frowning as she tried to think things through. Unfortunately all she could do was make up more and more horrific tortures for Jake.

The weather provided a fitting accompaniment to her mood. Long before she got to sleep a storm blew up from the south, setting the windows rattling in fury until a heavy deluge silenced everything in a thunderous downpour. Uneasily she tossed and turned, striving to summon from her childhood the secret pleasure in being snuggled up in the security of her bed, warm and safe and for once protected. It didn't work as well as it had when she was ten, but towards dawn she drifted off into sleep punctuated by dreams she couldn't recall when she woke up to a bleak day.

Alex had had an early lecture so she was gone by the time Cathy finally dragged herself out of bed. Some time during her restless night she had come to a decision; she would not think about Jake until she had finished the essay she was working on. When it was done she would work out how to tackle this latest development. It would not be easy to keep her mind clear but she was determined to do it. No more would she allow a man to clutter up her mind—not even the man she was in love with, the man who had as good as told her that he would humble her to the dust.

Her mouth firmed in a movement that Sir Peter's cohorts would have recognised. There was much more at stake here than a simple matter of pride. Jake had made it only too clear that he had no respect for her; so, she thought militantly, he was going to have to learn some. They would come together as equals, or not at all.

She drank a cup of cold coffee and had a hot shower then settled down to work, surfacing only for a sandwich at lunch time. Much later she heard Alex in the kitchen and came out, yawning.

'Gosh, it's been freezing, I don't think I've been warm for

a minute all day. What filthy weather. How's it going?' enquired Alex after a sapient glance.

'Not too bad, although what made me think I could understand the theory of economics I'll never know.'

Alex grinned. 'Natural inborn conceit, dear. What's for dinner?'

'Sausages.' Cathy looked around vaguely. 'I suppose I'd better do something about them.'

'As it is after seven, yes, you'd better. When you get down to work you really lose yourself, don't you?'

Cathy smiled. She had been rather surprised to discover her powers of concentration, and pleased. How astounded her long-suffering high-school teachers would be! As she prepared the meal she thought rather smugly that Jake would be surprised too; but that was being unfair and she knew it. In spite of his awesome capabilities he had never patronised her.

Firmly repressing any inclination to dwell on this subject, she set the table and joined Alex in the meal. Afterwards they played chess and then, yawning, went off to bed to the sound of even more rain and a wind keening around the corners of the house. Winter had definitely set in, a little early this year it seemed.

The next morning the rain had stopped but it was cuttingly cold, the sky polished blue by a wind straight off the Antarctic ice cap. Shivering, Cathy relit the gas heater and after seeing a profoundly reluctant Alex away went back to begin the final polishing of her essay.

She was about half-way through it when she realised that she could hear movements in the kitchen. Poor Alex must have forgotten the notes for the seminar she had been agitating over for the last month.

A glance at her watch revealed that it was past midday, so she got up thankfully and went down the hall, humming a little tune as she went.

Alex was standing by the kettle, and the look on her face stopped the cheerful little sound in mid-note.

CHAPTER TEN

CATHY'S hands flew to her heart, clenched protectively over its sudden painful throbbing. 'Alex, what—what is it?' she whispered.

'It—I heard a rumour. At least—it's not a rumour.' Alex's voice was flat, all emotion wiped from it. She looked away, and ran her tongue along her lips, before saying baldly, 'Jake's missing. Apparently he left on Friday night with a friend, in the friend's boat. They were going to sail across to Great Barrier and spend the weenend there, they were expected home late yesterday afternoon. But—they haven't made it back. You know what the weather's been like. The Air Force set up a search at first light. But they haven't found anything.'

'I see.' Cathy took a deep jagged breath. 'And it's definitely Jake?'

'I——' Alex grimaced. 'Yes.'

Cathy said nothing, but the look in her eyes made Alex give a frightened gasp. All light had fled from them, leaving them dead and cold, blindly unaware of anything but a pain so intense that she thought she might die of it.

'It's a lot of water to search,' Alex said, despising herself for holding out such faint cowardly comfort. 'Even if the boat went down they could be in a life-raft.'

Cathy looked up, that dead look fading into something like hope. 'I—if anyone could survive it, Jake will,' she said simply. 'But would a boat like that have a life-raft?'

'It should,' Alex said.

Cathy bit her lip. 'And wouldn't it have radio, or some means of communication?'

'Not necessarily, it might have been damaged or—or something.'

Cathy felt terror settle like a cold lump in the pit of her stomach. She whispered, 'He can't be dead. I would know, I'm sure.'

Brave words, but she had need of courage in the days that followed when all she could do was wait and hope. On the morning after that first day she rang Peter's number, but when a recorded voice asked her to give her name and message she put the receiver silently down. She had no official standing in Jake's life, and she knew that Peter would be too occupied coping with a distraught Emma to be able to deal with her.

Alex was kind and understanding, but after the second day even she could no longer hold out any hope. Wreckage from the boat had been found far to the north of their route and it was clear that they had hit some large object, either a whale or a container washed overboard from a ship. If by any remote chance either of the two men had survived the wreck they would be dead now from exposure.

'Unless they somehow made it to one of the islands,' Alex suggested diffidently.

'Surely if they managed to get to land they would have signalled?'

Alex said, 'There are a lot of islands . . .' Even she could not think of a reason why there would be no signal.

Cathy must have behaved with a certain approximation to her normal behaviour, because no one looked at her strangely as she went about her business. She felt very remote, imprisoned behind a necessary wall of reserve; she thought that if she allowed one thing to breach that wall it would crumble and carry her away with it. Several times she caught Alex watching her worriedly but she couldn't spare the energy to reassure her; it all went into keeping herself upright and behaving normally.

Somehow she felt that by refusing to consider the possibility of Jake's death, she was willing his survival. So she went to lectures and worked hard, smiled at people, even talked on occasions, and waited for the long, weary hours to go by, making the news bulletins the point of her existence.

After three days she rang Peter's number again, only to get the same message, but this time she gave the information and endured more waiting until he rang that night.

'Cathy,' he said, and she knew.

'Tell me.' Her voice was level yet Alex looked up sharply.

'Oh, God, Cath, we've just had news through from search headquarters. Sandy is alive.'

'And Jake?' She had to ask, even though she knew the answer.

'Jake died in the wreck. They hit a whale and Sandy got out but Jake was below. The boat went down in a matter of minutes. Jake never made it up on deck.'

Her breath came slowly between her lips. 'I see. Have they just found the other man?'

'Sandy? Yes. He was washed up on one of the islands off Whangarei Heads. He had some bushcraft but even so he's only just made it. He's in hospital with hypothermia.'

Still in that frozen voice, she asked, 'How is Emma?'

'Oh, God, she's in an awful state. She wouldn't take any sort of medication because of the baby, but she's asleep now. Sheer exhaustion.'

'I'm so sorry.'

There didn't seem to be anything else to say so she hung up and stood staring at the wall opposite, her eyes unfocused and waiting.

'Cathy?'

Alex took her arm and led her towards a seat. A moment later she pressed a glass of brandy into her hand. Automatically Cathy drank it, then gasped as the liquid burned its way down to her stomach.

The angry trill of the telephone barely impinged on her consciousness, for she was looking at a world without Jake, wondering in a pall of black despair how she was going to manage to survive in it.

When Alex came back she said gently, 'That was Peter. He was worried when you just hung up on him.'

'Poor Peter. Poor Emma.'

'Drink up the rest of that brandy,' Alex commanded gently, tears in her voice.

Docilely Cathy drained it. She was shivering when Alex told her to go to bed, and lay shivering all night through. She was still shivering when she heard the sound of breaking crockery in the kitchen, and a sudden glad cry from Alex, just before her flying footsteps raced towards Cathy's bedroom.

'It wasn't him!' she shouted incoherently. 'It wasn't him, Cathy! Jake's alive! It was the other man who died! It was on the news! Oh, Cathy, he's alive!'

It was too much. Cathy stared at Alex's excited face and burst into the tears which had been unable to penetrate the icy shell of her will all night.

Alex let out another whoop and sat down beside her, hugging her joyously as Cathy wept all the deep agony of mind and spirit away.

When at last the wrenching sobs had died Alex said briskly, 'Right, get up and have a shower, and I'll make us avocado toast with gruyere for breakfast. This is a day to celebrate.'

But before she followed this eminently satisfactory scenario Cathy rang Peter's number. She was considerably taken aback when Emma answered, but said nevertheless, 'I've just heard the good news, so I rang to tell you how happy I am for you.'

'That's very sweet of you.' Emma didn't have to say how she felt; her joy rang through her tones. 'Thank you, Cathy. It's been so terrible waiting for news—and even though we're so ecstatic, it's a truly tragic time for Jake's friend's family.'

'You've spoken to Jake?'

'Oh, yes, he rang as soon as he could. He's fine, just tired and wet and cold, he said. He's going to spend a couple of days in hospital in Whangarei, and Pete and I are going up this morning to see him. I'll tell him you called.'

'No, don't bother,' Cathy said hurriedly, recalling that last searing confrontation.

'Very well then.' Emma's voice was startled and for the first time really aware, as though through the euphoria of the moment memories of their relationship up until then had seeped. A little uncertainly she finished, 'Thank you for ringing, Cathy.'

And that, Cathy thought with wry resignation as she made some meaningless response, was that. Still, today nothing could damp her joy. Nothing could make her miserable ever again.

With a fully restored appetite she ate breakfast, her face suffused with an inner glow which gave her an almost ethereal beauty. At university she noticed the startled looks she was getting as her inner radiance registered, but although the whole place was humming with news of Jake's miraculous escape, no one thought to connect the two.

That joy lasted until a few days later when she heard on the grapevine that he was going to fly in to Auckland. Then, in spite of every warning instinct, she went out to the airport. It was ridiculous, and she scoffed at herself all the way there, but she had to see him just to reassure herself that he was all right. Nobody would see her. She would just look at him from a distance and once her hungry heart was satisfied, she would go home.

So when she got out of the car she tied a scarf around her brilliant hair before walking as inconspicuously as possible into the airport building. Always busy, it seemed more frenetic than usual with people scurrying around looking harassed. Her eyes noted a television crew and a woman reporter from one of the radio networks; presumably they were there to interview Jake.

And Emma was there, and Peter, and several other people who all looked excited and pleased. One of them was the woman Jake had escorted to the theatre. She and Emma clearly were on excellent terms. Cathy felt shut out, embarrassed by the fact that Jake had carefully kept her from any contact with his real life. She didn't know any of his friends. If he had tried, she thought sadly, he couldn't have made his feelings for her more plain. Like an old-fashioned mistress, kept distinct from all the really important things in his life.

But she couldn't even resent that just now. As the plane came down she watched with bated breath, stupidly terrified that death, balked of its prey for once, might try again.

Of course the aircraft made a perfect landing. There was a buzz of chatter, but Cathy's eyes were fixed almost painfully on the door. Jake was the last person out, attended by a hostess who had her face raised worshipfully to his.

Cathy's eyes devoured him. From this distance she couldn't see much more than the shape of his face. Certainly she couldn't tell whether he was tired or not for he walked across the tarmac in his normal loose-jointed panther stride, without any evidence of his exhausting ordeal. So intent was she on watching him that it wasn't until he had gone out of sight that she realised all of the people who waited for him had left the room, even the television crew and the reporters.

She got herself a cup coffee and drank it without tasting

it, lost in the complicated emotions she had felt on seeing him again. She had been astounded to find resentment there, because he had the power to make her as unhappy as she had been those terrifying days before he had been found, and a great surge of love and longing, and at the bottom, a certain peace.

It was this she welcomed, this she strove to retain. She had to develop some kind of armour against the empty years which stretched ahead, their darkness lightened only by her memory of how truly hopeless everything had been when she believed him dead.

At last, with her shoulders braced against the world, she left the cafeteria and walked across the floor of the arrival hall towards the doors.

The sound of her name whipped her head around. At the sight of the man who stood there she whispered, 'No. Oh, no . . .' and looked huntedly around for a way to escape.

Too late. His lean elegant hands closed on her arms, holding her still, a rigid, resistant figure, her face chiselled from marble.

Jake said angrily, 'What the hell have you been doing to yourself?'

'Nothing.' She tried to duck her head away from his scrutiny but his incredulous gaze swept her comprehensively, noting the pale face dominated by tired eyes where the shadows of pain and grief still lingered.

'Cathy,' he said harshly. 'Why weren't you waiting with the others? I missed——' And then, his glance sharpening, 'Was this for me?'

And because she loved him and she had thought him dead she no longer wanted to protect herself. The fear of rejection which had coloured her life for so many years seemed an insignificant thing.

Tears welled up in her eyes. 'I thought you were dead,' she said desolately.

'No. No, you didn't. You'd have known. Just as I'd know if you died.' His arms contracted, pulling her against the warmth of his body. His cheek came down on her head. For long moments they stood clasped together until he said in a thick voice, 'Cathy, come home with me.' Then, over her head, 'Peter, you go on home; I'm going with Cathy.'

Emma's voice was soft and indulgent. 'Just see that he gets straight to bed, Cathy. He won't admit it, but he's exhausted.'

She didn't say anything, didn't even nod. Her heart was hammering so hard she thought she might die. Mistily she smiled into the damp wool of his jersey.

They walked hand in hand to her car; she wondered whether he would want to drive but a look at his exhausted face gave her an answer. Indeed, he made no attempt to take the wheel, but relaxed back into the front seat, leaning his head on to the rest, eyes closing. His profile was as hawkish as ever but now she could see traces of his ordeal in new lines at the corners of his eyes and in the pallor beneath the tanned skin. He looked exhausted, as though it was only will-power which gave him the stamina to keep going.

However, he managed to stay awake until they reached the block of flats where he lived. As she locked the car Cathy thought worriedly that he really should still be under medical supervision, but when she said this he said wearily, 'That's all been taken take care of. At Whangarei they hooked me up to every machine in the damned place! I'm tired, that's all. All I want is a shower and bed, in that order.'

And that was what he had. While he showered she made a pot of tea, persuaded him to drink a cup, and when it was gone she bullied him into bed. Unselfconsciously he stripped off the robe he wore and dropped it on to the floor.

Cathy's mouth dried. Thin and weary though he was, he

was still the most beautiful man she had ever seen in her life, and the only naked one. She looked up at his face and saw a wry smile twist his lips.

'I'm not going to be much good to you until I've had a decent night's sleep, I'm afraid,' he said.

Her voice was husky as she said with an attempt at her usual pertness, 'I've never thought of you as a stud, Jake.'

'No, it would have been easier for both of us if you had,' he replied obliquely. 'Why don't you come to bed? You look as though you could do with some rest too.'

She blushed, but his gaze held nothing but calm enquiry, and she suddenly nodded. As if he understood her shyness he got into the bed, disposing his length between the sheets with an unconscious little grunt of pleasure which twisted her heartstrings. She pulled off her clothes, sliding in beside him with her pulses beating so fast that she heard nothing but their pounding.

He turned towards her and enfolded her.

'So small . . .' His voice trailed away but after a second he finished, 'So sweet . . .'

And almost immediately his regular breathing told her that he was asleep.

Astonishingly she soon followed him, her heart singing with a happiness so intense it was like a pain in her body.

She woke to that same feeling, a soaring joy like nothing she had ever experienced before. She should have been frightened, because there was no way she could control this emotion, it obeyed its own laws.

Always before she had been wary of allowing herself to feel, starting perhaps from the trauma of her father's death. Too young to have any conception of mortality, she knew that he had left her, and she had felt betrayed. Then had come her mother's marriage and subsequent defection. More betrayal, more rejection.

Even the marriage to Trent . . . She had thought herself

in control there, too. When he made it patently obvious that she could not control him, she had left him with little more than ruffled pride.

But now . . . She turned to look at the man whose arm was flung across her body. He was still asleep, the strong clear-cut lines of his face blurred slightly by exhaustion and the villainous beginnings of a beard. He even looked slightly raffish, her elegant Jake.

Smiling, her whole body lax with love, she snuggled under the blanket and curved into the lean, exciting heat of him. He made an indeterminate noise and his arm tightened.

She felt him waken. It was an instantaneous process, about as far removed from her reluctant resurgence as anything could be. One moment he was lying loosely against her, the next he was vibrant with life, the cool powerful brain humming over at top speed.

'Cathy?'

'Mm?' Purposely she kept her eyes shut. She was afraid of what she might see in that beloved face.

'Look at me,' he commanded quietly.

Her lashes quivered, but a note in his voice brought them up. She peeped out at him, surprising a smile on his face that made her heart stand still.

'I think,' he said, 'we had better get married.'

Her lashes flew up. She stared at him in such patent astonishment that he gave a twisted smile. It didn't soften the fierce determination in his face. Unconsciously her teeth began to worry her lip.

'Don't,' he said, and pulled her across so that he could touch the maltreated flesh with a gentle finger. 'You always chew your lip when you're afraid. Well, you have a right to be worried, I suppose, because I'm not going to let you go. When I was out in that freezing hellhole only one thing kept me going, and that was the vision of your smiling face. I

promised myself that when I got back I'd have you again,
make you mine until you would never be able to see another
man.' He gave a soft breathy laugh and held his fingers like
a bar across her protesting mouth.

'Yes, I know it sounds macho and chauvinist and down-
right primitive, but with you that's how I am. It's shameful
that it took the imminent danger of death to make me admit
that I haven't forgotten a thing about the only time we
made love. Or that I haven't wanted another woman since
the first time I saw you.'

He paused, collecting his thoughts. Cathy lay like a
prisoner, afraid to move in case he stopped long enough to
remember that this was the enemy he was talking to.

'That first glimpse of you,' he said reminiscently, 'was a
photograph. Peter had a whole album of them and I was
leafing through it one day. I asked who the pocket Venus
was and he told me; he spoke of you with such affection that
I was appalled and astonished to find I was jealous. Of a
photograph. I never forgot your face. I'd like to think that
when Emma started writing me furious letters about you I
came back out of brotherly protectiveness, but that would
be incorrect. Not that I admitted that I wanted to see if the
sulky beauty in the snapshots was as desirable in the flesh.
No, that would have been giving too much importance to a
woman.'

He was tracing the shape of her mouth with a very sure,
very gentle finger. Cathy lay very still, her whole
concentration bent on what he was saying yet violently
aware of the hard length of his body, the heat from his skin,
the faint masculine scent of him.

He said abruptly, 'Then I met you, and you were everything I'd dreamed of, and I wanted you in a way I'd never
wanted anyone else before. It told myself it was nothing,
just lust, that you were the woman who was sleeping with
my brother-in-law, that you were a promiscuous little bitch,

hard enough to blackmail Addison into marrying you—but when I was over at the island I found myself making excuses for you. Perhaps you loved your grandfather and it had been some mistaken form of loyalty which made you fall in with his plans for Addison, perhaps you slept with Peter because you loved him and the only way you could show your sympathy for him was in bed . . . There are women like that, just as there are men who can divorce tenderness from desire.'

His voice was sombre, yet there was a note of pain in it which widened Cathy's eyes. She looked up into a face suddenly drawn and intent, and said with difficulty, 'You don't need to tell me this. It doesn't matter.'

'I think it does.' He cupped her cheek with his hands, the long fingers sliding smoothly over the warm contours. His index finger stroked down the vulnerable length of her throat; at the base it stopped, and his hand wrapped around her neck.

He bent and kissed her mouth, fiercely, trying to purge himself of some dark emotion. Cathy winced but opened for him, as she always had, always would.

Against her lips he said, 'But the thought of you being in love with bloody Peter made me savage. I wanted to hurt you, bitterly, brutally. I wanted to keep you with me, carry you off somewhere and make you love me, force you to submit, take everything you had to give, and I told myself that this was how sirens were, they degraded where they obsessed. Except that the more I saw of you the less I believed what I'd been told. Oh, you're far from being an angel. You were a little thoughtless, a little too fond of having your own way, but you were tender-hearted and gentle, and you made me realise why men fall in love with totally unsuitable women.'

'Am I that?' she asked in a shaken voice. 'Totally unsuitable?'

The pain was incredible. When he had said 'fall in love' she had had a moment of ecstasy so exquisite that she had felt pierced by joy, ravished by it, and then had come the cruel ending.

'Oh, yes. Totally, wildly unsuitable. In every way.'

'I see.' Her voice was like the days ahead, grey and flat, lacking life, lacking colour.

'So why did I fall in love with you? Why am I determined to marry you?'

She exploded into action, shouting words she didn't hear, hitting him with small fists which stung as she spat out that she wouldn't marry him if he were the last man on earth, and he flung his head back and laughed and crushed the words to nothingness on her mouth and pinned her wrists above her head, holding her wildly thrashing body imprisoned until, panting and speechless, she stared at him.

He was not looking at her face. Her antics had stripped the sheet and blanket from the top of the bed and she was lying exposed to his eyes like a slave girl in the bed of her conqueror.

He said unevenly. 'You enchant me. I look at you and all I can think about is you. And this.'

The movement was so swift she was pinned to the mattress before she could make any outcry. With pagan, brutal power he entered her, and she, who had always thought she was cold, found that her body was ready.

He said in an appalled voice. 'My God! Cathy——'

'No! Don't——' Impelled by instinct, she wrapped her legs around his, clamping on to him with desperate urgency. Her hands tightened across the corded muscles in his back; she moved, lifting her hips, thrusting, and he gave a tortured sound and established a driving rhythm which penetrated right to the depths, so that when at last he shuddered and gasped her name she was as lost to reality as he was.

He collapsed, all his proud male strength sapped, and rolled on to his side, scooping her with him so that she was half sprawled and exhausted as she lay listening to the thunder of his heart slow down, smiling to herself with the secret feminine smile which all women know.

When at last he was able to speak he said quietly, 'Out there, in the rain and the wind and the sea, almost certain that I was going to die, I kept thinking of something Peter told me. He said he'd never touched you, and he followed that up by trying to convince me that Addison had never slept with you either. I didn't believe that, because you had given yourself to me with all the fire and passion of an experienced woman. I have dreamed so often of the way you were, so ardent that you burned me up, but I've never allowed myself to wonder why afterwards you seemed so bewildered by your own response. Was it true, Cathy? Was Peter telling the truth?'

'Yes.'

'But Addison was your husband. And a normal man.'

'A very normal man,' she said wryly. 'But Trent is every bit as stubborn and as autocratic as you are. And he was already in love with Melly.'

'You didn't know that before you engineered that marriage.'

She was pleased because it was a statement, not a question. Her finger touched the damp curls which covered his muscular chest, threading through the fine hair in a meandering pattern. 'No, I didn't, or I'd have never put him in the position where my grandfather was able to blackmail him into marrying me. Trent had just started up his electronics business and my grandfather controlled his supplies.'

'And he threatened to cut them off.' His voice was very level, almost as though he was angry.

She nodded, her eyes following her vagrant finger.

'I don't think that he'd have given in even then, only he had all his workers to consider. But when we were married he made it quite obvious that it was to be in name only. Jake, I don't think I'll ever be able to forgive myself for what I did. I was so arrogant and stupid, I thought that because I was infatuated with him he had to love me. He and Melly lost three years of happiness because I was so stupidly, selfishly set on having my own way.'

'Hush,' he said gently. 'If Addison and his wife can forgive you, why can't you?'

She gulped and burrowed her head into his chest, furious with the tears that refused to be denied any longer. 'I don't know why they have, but I didn't know, until I met you, what it was like.'

'What what was like?'

'Being in love. Loving someone so much that you feel like half a person without them.'

In a voice she didn't recognise he asked, 'Is that how you feel with me?'

She nodded, welcoming the abrasion of his chest hair against her skin, because she didn't dare look up at him.

'Oh, my dearest heart,' he said roughly, 'I know. It happened to both of us. Why do you think I've been so bloody-minded to you? Because I fell in love with a spoiled selfish little bitch with no morals and the most wicked smile in all the world—Cathy, stop hiding down there! I want to see your face.'

She lifted it, transformed into a heart-shaking beauty by the power of love reciprocated, gazing misty-eyed into his saturnine features. He swallowed, and whispered her name, and kissed her, deeply as love, sweetly as desire, enabled by love to claim a mastery she would never otherwise have granted him.

'Did I hurt you?' he said roughly. 'I can't believe that I

took you so cruelly.'

'It didn't hurt.' She was surprised.

His hand stroked through the damp tangle of her hair, glowing red and bronze and gold over his arm. 'Cathy, that first time we made love, I had the strangest feeling—was it the first time ever for you?'

She nodded.

He closed his eyes, saying in a shaken voice, 'I was so strung out with frustration and passion that it must have been a horrifying experience for you. I thought—well, you know what I thought. But even if you had been experienced I can make no excuse for the way I forced you, except to say that you have the most powerful effect on me. Because I've just done it again. It won't happen any more, I promise you.'

Pressing her hot cheek against his chest she muttered, 'I liked it. It wasn't at all what I'd imagined my first experience would be like but I was carried away by the storm—it seemed right, somehow. Just now, too.'

He laughed, using a long forefinger to tip her face upwards so that he could look into it. 'Most virgins, so one hears, have to be persuaded and coaxed into bed, and then there is a long, slow, tender, painstaking initiation process to go through. I suppose, dearest heart, that it is par for the course that you should be so completely different.' His eyes narrowed, brilliant chips of aquamarine behind his lashes as his gaze drifted down. 'You are completely different from any other woman I've ever met. Sleek and sweet and fiery, with a tang all of your own. You don't even care about this freakish brain of mine, do you?'

'Freakish?' She was inclined to be indignant. 'Who told you it was freakish? One of the tutors at university said that no one even knows what the normal range of human intelligence is, so how can it be freakish?' She reached up and kissed his smiling mouth firmly. 'You are just very intelligent. And sexy. And kind. And arrogant and bossy. And I love you. Rather more. I think, than life itself.'

'Oh, my dear.' His voice shook, telling her how much the artless declaration had moved him. 'That's more than I deserve. I behaved like a swine because I didn't want to love you.'

She looked up, her eyes very candid. 'I know. But why? Because you knew how much Emma would hate it?'

He sighed. 'Yes. Partly. I knew that she was unstable, she's had difficulty ever since our parents were killed.'

'Perhaps,' Cathy suggested, 'she was afraid that anyone she loved might abandon her as it seemed her parents did.'

'That was part of the problem, anyway. She's always been possessive, but I thought when she was married her jealousy would fade. However, that's no excuse. I should have realised what was likely to happen and been a little less credulous, but Peter wouldn't deny that he was your lover, and I resented the fact that I had only to look at you and every principle I had went down the drain. I used Emma's neurotic fear to armour myself against admitting that I wanted you, and by doing so I increased the strain on her and made you utterly miserable. But I did not set you up the night we came back from the island.'

The anger in his voice was raw and intense, directed solely at himself. Cathy kissed him gently.

'I know,' she said.

He gave a short surprised laugh. 'You have more faith in me than I deserve. It was when she tried to make you believe I'd plotted with her that I realised how close to a breakdown she was. When Peter finally came home after doing some hard thinking he and I managed to get her to admit that she needed help. He convinced her that he'd never slept with you, and agreed to go with her to therapy.

When she admitted that she had used her breakdown as a threat, I knew she was going to be all right.'

'Was that when you tracked me down to the island?'

'Yes.' His voice was muffled and he kissed the soft line of her mouth with a slow stinging thoroughness. 'I'm not proud of myself for the way I behaved, and the only excuse I can give is that I was still fighting a rearguard action against loving you. Even after we'd made love, even though it was the most earth-shattering experience I've ever had, I still wouldn't admit that I felt anything more for you than the most irresistible lust.'

'So you went away to get me out of your hair.' Her voice was acid.

'Only to find that you were entangled in my heart. Without you my life turned into a wasteland, without colour and brightness and warmth. Because I'm a stubborn bastard I resented that, blaming you; I came back here determined to coax you into my bed. I didn't look beyond that until I almost died, and then I realised that my stupidity might have cost me the one thing I wanted above all others.'

'I learned to love you on the island,' she told him slowly, recognising the note of vulnerability in the deep tones. 'You were all that I had ever looked for. I wanted to make you happy, give you everything you wanted . . . Then, when you—when you——'

'Betrayed you,' he supplied roughly.

'Even then, I couldn't believe that you hadn't felt something for me. It had been so strong—I felt that you couldn't have kept it up so consistently if it was all a lie.'

'You were wiser than I. Because of course you were right. It wasn't a lie.'

'Then you left, and it hurt so much I had to try to forget you, to suppress all the pain and all the happy memories. It didn't work but I was determined. When you came back I had to face the fact that it was far from over, and if I was going to keep some control of the situation, I'd better work out just how I did feel about you. Which reminds me . . .' She turned fiercely to him. 'Just who was the woman you took to the theatre?'

He laughed, flinging his head back and scooping her so closely that she was shocked anew by his lean readiness. 'A friend of Emma's; you'll like her. I do.'

She allowed him to get away with that. 'Do you like me?'

'You drive me mad. Yes, I like you. I love you, I adore you, I have hungered and thirsted and yearned for you, and now you are mine and I feel the way Alexander must have felt when he realised that he had a whole world out there to conquer. Now, about this slow, tender initiation I was talking about . . . I don't want you feeling that you've missed out on every woman's birthright . . .'

She grinned, that wicked smile he knew so well, and bent her head to kiss him just above one of the flat male nipples.

'I'm ready if you are,' she said.

It was, so the gossips said, the most interesting wedding of the year. Probably of the decade. Not only was the bride given away by her ex-husband, who looked, as far as his sardonic cast of features revealed, as proud as any doting father, but the groom was supported by his brother-in-law, commonly rumoured to be the bride's former lover.

As if this was not enough, the spouses of both these men were very much members of the party, both pregnant, and both looking quite cheerful about the whole affair. Those who had gone to the church hoping for some juicy titbit of gossip switched their attention from Melly Addison's radiant face to that of the bridegroom's sister. *Everyone* knew for a fact that she and Cathy had come to blows on more than one occasion . . .

But once again they were balked of legitimate prey.
Emma too appeared cheerful and completely contented
with the whole situation.

The groom, so they decided afterwards, was his usual
assured self, handsome and quite impossible to read, except
for one moment when he turned as Cathy came up the aisle
of the chapel at her old school. And then even the most
hardened of gossips found themselves blinking and
consulting their handkerchiefs, for in that instant they saw
all his love blaze forth, transforming the hard dominance of
his face with complete happiness.

And the bride, small and erect in an ivory silk dress which
set off her beautiful skin and hair—tamed for once beneath a
netted snood dotted with seed pearls—well, the bride
looked at him as if he were all that she would ever need in
this life or any other.

One unsentimental matron found a line of Herrick's
poetry click into her brain. That most frivolous of poets
said it exactly. *All love, all liking, all delight.* She sighed, and
hated herself for the pang of envy that tore through
her.

Later, when all the food had been eaten and the
champagne drunk, when at last they were alone, Jake said
words from an older poet.

'Such a "*sweet red splendid kissing mouth*" you have, my
darling,' he murmured as the ivory silk slithered to the
floor. Beneath it Cathy wore a slim slip and lacy
underpinnings, as brief as they were pretty. Excitement
coursed through her like rivers of fire from a volcano
blazing across a night landscape, beautiful and awe-
inspiring; she put up her hands and began to undo the
buttons of his shirt, but her fingers were trembling so much
that she couldn't manage it.

'Frightened?'

She shook her head. 'How can I be afraid? It's you,' she said simply.

His hand held hers against his chest. Beneath the splayed fingers she could feel the thunder of his heart as it picked up speed. It gave her confidence.

'I love you,' she whispered.

'And I you.' The dark head bent; he picked her up and carried her across to the wide bed where he set her on her feet and with skilful fingers rid her of all her clothing.

Reverently he touched her, his dark face absorbed and intent, his fingers slightly trembling. His regard lifted to her grave, smiling face and he said in an astonished voice, 'I love you and I need you, and until I met you I had never needed a person in my life. I think that's why I was so hard on us both.'

'And I had spent my life expecting to be rejected.' Her fingers pulled the material of his shirt free from the buttons. She leaned forward and put her cheek against his chest, smiling again as the speed of his heart threatened to deafen her. 'That's why I couldn't believe that there was any future for us. I think it's probably why I didn't even try to correct your misapprehensions about me.'

'I doubt if I'd have believed you.' His voice was deep and hard with control. Then it snapped and he caught her and held her with passionate fury against him. 'I promise to believe everything you ever tell me in the future,' he whispered. 'My dearest love, my heart's sweet companion, I'd trust you with my life.'

She struggled free but only to kiss him, her mouth supplicant and eager beneath his. 'And I've trusted you with my happiness,' she whispered. 'Jake, I love you.

He made a strange sound deep in his throat, picked her up and slid her beneath the sheet, and as she lay watching, pulled off his clothes.

Cathy's eyes pleasured themselves with the sight of him, lean and strong and perfect, hers for ever. This she thought, as he came down to her, oh, this was worth all that she had suffered. Love was truly its own reward.

Harlequin Presents

Coming Next Month

Available in February wherever paperback books are sold, or through Harlequin Reader Service:

In the U.S.
901 Fuhrmann Blvd.
P.O. Box 1397
Buffalo, N.Y 14240-1397

In Canada
P.O. Box 603
Fort Erie, Ontario
L2A 5X3

A compelling novel of deadly revenge and passion
from Harlequin's bestselling international
romance author Penny Jordan

POWER PLAY

Eleven years had passed but the
terror of that night was something
Pepper Minesse would never
forget. Fueled by revenge against
the four men who had brutally
shattered her past, she set in
motion a deadly plan to destroy
their futures.

Available in February!

 Harlequin Books®

HPP-1A

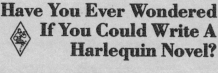

Have You Ever Wondered If You Could Write A Harlequin Novel?

Here's great news—Harlequin is offering a series of cassette tapes to help you do just that. Written by Harlequin editors, these tapes give practical advice on how to make your characters—and your story—come alive. There's a tape for each contemporary romance series Harlequin publishes.

Mail order only

All sales final

Harlequin Superromance®

LET THE GOOD TIMES ROLL...

Add some Cajun spice to liven up your New Year's celebrations and join Superromance for a romantic tour of the rich Acadian marshlands and the legendary Louisiana bayous.

Starting in January 1990, we're launching CAJUN MELODIES, a three-book tribute to the fun-loving people who've enriched America by introducing us to crawfish étouffé and gumbo, zydeco music and the Saturday night party, the *fais-dodo*. And learn about loving, Cajun-style, as you meet the tall, dark, handsome men who win their ladies' hearts with a beautiful, haunting melody....

Book One: *Julianne's Song*, January 1990
Book Two: *Catherine's Song*, February 1990
Book Three: *Jessica's Song*, March 1990

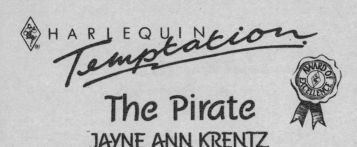

HARLEQUIN Temptation

The Pirate
JAYNE ANN KRENTZ

At the heart of every powerful romance story lies a
legend. There are many romantic legends and
countless modern variations on them, but they all
have one thing in common: They are tales of brave,
resourceful women who must gentle and tame the
powerful, passionate men who are their true mates.

The enormous appeal of Jayne Ann Krentz lies in
her ability to create modern-day versions of these
classic romantic myths, and her LADIES AND
LEGENDS trilogy showcases this talent. Believing
that a storyteller who can bring legends to life
deserves special attention, Harlequin has chosen
the first book of the trilogy—THE PIRATE—to
receive our Award of Excellence. Look for it in
February.

AE-PIR-1